A CHRISTMAS MYSTERY IN VENICE AND OTHER WINTER TALES

3 SHORT STORIES

ADRIANA LICIO

The Home Travellers
Press

A CHRISTMAS MYSTERY IN VENICE AND OTHER WINTER TALES
3 Short Stories in the *Homeswappers Mysteries* series
By Adriana Licio

Edition I
Copyright 2022 © Adriana Licio

All rights reserved. This book or any portion thereof may not be reproduced or used in any manner whatsoever without the express written permission of the author except for the use of brief quotations in book reviews.

This is a work of fiction. Names, businesses, places, events and incidents are either the products of the author's imagination or used in a fictitious manner. All the characters in this book are fictitious, and any resemblance to actual persons, living or dead, is purely coincidental.

Cover by **Wicked Smart Design**
Editing by **Alison Jack**

To my Frodo,
My canine friend, fellow walker and inspirer of all sorts of adventures.
You're deeply missed.

To Antonietta,
Who opened her heart and home to welcome us throughout the summer
and autumn of 2022.
At times a sister, at others a mother,
A precious friend always.

To Giovanni,
In my meanderings right and left,
Up and down in life,
You teach me to be peaceful in the here and now;
To dance in the storms;
To take in whatever the world offers.

CONTENTS

1. A TUSCAN THREAT	1
2. A CHRISTMAS MYSTERY IN VENICE	37
3. DEVILISH DEEDS IN THE ALPS	73
More Books From Adriana Licio	143
About the Author	145
THE MYSTERY BEFORE CHRISTMAS	147

1. A TUSCAN THREAT

THE HOMESWAPPERS MYSTERIES - A SHORT STORY

1

A STRANGE INVITATION

"Remind me, why are we doing this?" Etta harrumphed as the rain rattled against her waterproof coat and rucksack, dripping down her neck and soaking her jumper, fogging her glasses. How could humans have reached the 21st century without inventing wipers for spectacles?

"Because Mrs Strikeheaven", Dora scrambled up the path through the contorted forest, the last few leaves hanging on to the chestnut and oak trees for dear life, "heard about your extraordinary sleuthing skills and asked for your help."

As usual, Dora was as happy, chirpy and cheerful as if it were a fine spring day. Etta's question had been rhetorical. She knew very well why they were heading to the old Mosceta Mill in Alpi Apuane, a lesser-known part of Tuscany, but sarcasm would be lost on her friend, the naive people-pleaser.

Thunder rumbled through the forest, causing the two women and their canine companion to retract their heads into their shoulders like tortoises. Were they going to be roasted alive by lightning before they'd even reached their destination?

"Not that far now," Dora repeated what she'd said 20 minutes earlier. Napoleon, the noble Basset Hound affectionately known as Leon, cast a droopy glance of disbelief her way. He was not that easily fooled. "In any case," Dora added, "it would take longer to go back now. It's only an hour's hike."

"This isn't a hike, it's a mud bath." Etta lifted her boots one at a time from the gloopy slime to emphasise her point. Although Leon had a soft spot for Dora, the gentler of the two sexagenarian bipeds he had taken responsibility for, he had to agree with Etta this time. His paws were sinking so deeply into the thick layer of mud, it had reached his belly. And whose idea had it been to clothe him in a ridiculous yellow raincoat? Not only was it no protection against the pouring rain, but it made his long body look like an Italian school bus. What if one of his many fans were to see him?

"What was I thinking?" Etta muttered as she trudged on. When Mrs Strikeheaven had declared she needed the help of an analytical mind, Etta's first question had been, "What's happened?"

"Nothing, actually," Mrs Strikeheaven had replied. Apparently, that wasn't the point. The point was, nothing had happened... *yet*. "But," Mrs Strikeheaven's voice was throaty and deep, "the mill's atmosphere changed all of a sudden when we started to prepare for the annual Halloween party. I'm full of foreboding. Please come, otherwise the consequences will be terrible."

Etta would have dismissed her as a hysterical timewaster, had the woman's tone not been so rational. And Halloween in the charming sunny hills of Tuscany had seemed like a grand idea.

"Sunny and charming, my eye!" Etta muttered, narrowly avoiding a muddy slide down a particularly steep slope. Alpi Apuane was obviously not the Chianti wine region; it was somewhere far wilder. What lay in store for them in Col di Favilla, the remote village they were heading towards?

1. A Tuscan Threat

WHEN THE RAIN FINALLY STOPPED, THE TWO WOMEN WERE SURPRISED to find themselves encircled by stone buildings that seemed to be almost a natural continuation of the forest. One towering tree trunk revealed itself to be the bell tower of a church, once Etta had wiped her large red-framed glasses yet again.

Before she could say anything, Dora was dancing a jig towards the building. "A little church!" she exclaimed happily.

"We're searching for our overnight accommodation, not touring the sights of Florence," grumbled Etta, unmoved. "I hope it's not a hollowed-out oak tree."

"Come here, Etta," Dora was peering through a window. "There's a beautiful dedication," and without pausing, she read out loud, "Throughout life, we're rarely aware that we receive much more than we give. It's only through gratitude that our lives get richer. Thanks go to all those who contribute to keeping ancient places alive."

"That church," a voice from behind them made them both jump, "was reduced to a mass of ruins, denuded of all its memories, statues and paintings, and left vulnerable to the fury of the elements and the scavengers." The voice belonged to a tall, sturdy man. Blond and tanned, he had a deeply thoughtful expression in his grey eyes.

He bent to his knees and called Leon over. "And what's this?" he asked the dog, laughing at the yellow waterproof.

"He's ashamed of it," confessed Dora. "I'm afraid it was my idea, and it didn't even prove particularly useful." Leon glared at her with his best I-told-you-so expression. "But the church," Dora chirped. "It looks fine and well taken care of to me."

"That's only thanks to the citizens of Col di Favilla. When the village was abandoned, they moved all over Tuscany, but their hearts stayed here. They raised the money to restore the church back in 1983."

5

The church stood a little apart from the rest of the village. The two friends could see some stone houses with slate shingle roofs, almost swallowed by the forest. Most were ruins with their roofs fallen in, but a few had been restored with new wooden doors and shutters.

"Does anyone live here?" Etta asked.

"I do," the man said simply, "and some of my fellow citizens are returning. Some only at weekends, but we're not letting our village disappear."

"That's wonderful!" Ever the romantic, Dora clasped her hands together. She couldn't resist a heart-warming story, no matter how brief.

"You live here?" The pragmatic Etta didn't share her friend's rose-tinted glasses. "I don't see a single shop, and it's over an hour's walk to civilisation."

The man looked uncertain, as if confused by the contrast between the two women. Somewhat reluctantly, he continued his explanation.

"There's a shorter route, passable with a 4 by 4. I take it you walked from Isola Santa?"

"A shorter route?" Etta cried, the cold and dampness penetrating her body now that they had stopped marching. The man nodded; Etta looked at Dora accusingly. Dora's eyes were fixed on the ground, her cheeks on fire.

"Well, it wouldn't have been the same to arrive in a car..."

"You knew? We're all going to catch pneumonia in this forgotten place just because of your misplaced sentimentality? Someone stop me from hurting her in front of the House of the Lord!"

The man glared at Etta. "This is not a forgotten place. Actually, it is very much alive to its current and former citizens."

"If there's not a grocery or bakery, it's not a village," Etta snapped. The cold, not to mention Dora's betrayal, made her even more despondent than usual. "At least you should know where Mosceta Mill is..."

"So that's where you're heading. I should have known – that American, bringing her commercial charade over here!"

"I take it you mean the Halloween party?"

"Of course, I do. Those traditions are fine on the other side of the Atlantic, but they do not belong here!"

"Come on!" A high voice from the other side of the church took them all by surprise. "You shouldn't discourage our visitors, and any party is good if it draws people to Col di Favilla."

A bright-faced young woman with light brown hair and shining blue eyes joined them. She spoke with the typical Tuscan accent, turning the k sound into an h.

"Benedetta," the man flushed a little, Etta didn't know whether in anger or shame, "we should strive to keep our own traditions alive before all this commercial stuff. Anyway, these ladies are enquiring about the mill. They must be Adele's guests."

"And mine," the young woman smiled into the sulky face of the man.

"Come on," he pleaded. "You can't be into this pumpkin-led foolery, too."

"Actually, I've just left my pumpkin carving duties to see if our friends had arrived. It will be delightful to see the autumnal village glowing."

"It won't be."

"Of course, it will. I... actually, we will make sure of it."

Etta, Dora and Leon found their eyes moving from the woman to the man and back again. It was like being at a tennis match.

"You should lend a hand," Benedetta continued.

"Never!" he yelled. "And if you dare spoil my village with those silly Jack-o'-Lanterns, I'll remove them immediately."

"You'll do no such thing!" Benedetta's voice rose too. "We have permission from Stazzema's mayor, so you can't spoil our party. Just because you're so sad, you have no right to impose unhappiness all around."

The man was now red in the face and sweating as if it were high summer. Etta and Dora feared he would launch himself on to Benedetta at any moment.

"I'm not sad, Ms Know-it-all, I just respect a place and its traditions. And I came back here from Milan because I love the peace and tranquillity, two things that have nothing to do with sadness. But that's something you loud folks with your crowded soulless parties will never understand. Don't you dare spoil this place, do you hear me?"

Leon decided enough was enough. He did not like humans barking; it was OK for dogs, particularly those with a melodious voice like his, but an abominable trait in bipeds. And more importantly, it was time to find a cosy place to warm up in with some decent food. He slid his long body between the two quarrellers and treated the man to the trademark "Woof, woof, WOOF!" that had proved so effective in getting the attention of humans in the past. Then he uttered the same in the direction of the woman.

"Just what we need, a noisy dog." The man wasn't about to apply the brakes; he was on a roll. "Make sure your party is well away from my place, and that your guests don't go around damaging our village."

Finally satisfied, he turned his back on them all and disappeared into a copse of chestnut trees.

"I'm so sorry you had to arrive to this…"

"Oh no, I enjoyed it," confessed Etta. Used to being labelled unreasonable, cranky and irascible, she was happy to hand the baton over to someone else.

"Oh," Dora admonished, "how can you condone such a temper, especially in a thoughtful young man?"

"He must be thoughtful to decide to live here all by himself," Benedetta agreed.

"You're confusing thoughtfulness with misanthropy," Etta said to the young woman. "He certainly doesn't seem to like you."

"Which is a pity, as there's not exactly an abundance of people around."

"Is he the only person living in Col di Favilla permanently?"

"You're soaked. Let's go home and I'll tell you more on the way."

"Is it far?"

"No, just at the end of this path… past Ugo's house, I'm afraid."

"Is that the man we just…"

"Indeed." Benedetta pointed towards a few steps carved into the stone, leading to a track overgrown with brambles and paved with leaves. "Can we even call it a path?" She laughed. "But to answer your question, there's Silvana, our… our… neighbour. And Piero and Francesca Puppa, two former teachers who decided to retire here. Then there are the people who only spend part of the year here, like Mr Brandibaldi, a banker from Florence, and his fiancée, a typical socialite…"

"A socialite? In Col di Favilla?" Etta said.

"Hmm, yes – a socialite who has to comply with the wishes of her husband-to-be, at least until they're married. And," she said, pointing to a large square building in a clearing, a brook running by its side, "this is home."

"Oh no!" cried Etta and Leon in unison. Well, Leon didn't exactly cry, but he wore the same look of despair as Etta. In response to Benedetta's puzzled expression, Etta nodded her head towards her friend. Dora seemed petrified, as motionless as a victim of Medusa, her hands clasped as she gazed in awe at the stone stairs decorated with carved pumpkins glowing against the dark of the forest and the cheerless sky. "That's unfortunate."

"What?" Benedetta now looked horrified.

"She's in ecstasy, like St Teresa of Avila. Nothing can reach her. She's been known to stay like that for days."

Leon sank to the ground, attempting to cover his forehead with his paws.

"You two are pulling my leg," the young woman chuckled. "It can't be that bad." And almost as if she had heard through her rapture, Dora began coming back to her senses.

"Did you make the decorations?" she asked Benedetta dreamily.

"Yes... are they really that bad?"

"Bad? They're enchanting! The millstone is the ideal backdrop, and the chestnut trees and the brook make it perfect. I've always dreamed of celebrating Halloween, but Don Peppino – our Priest back home in Castelmezzano – is strongly against it."

"We should send Don Peppino and Ugo on a trip together," suggested Benedetta, chuckling again. "Preferably at the end of October so we can do as we wish."

"I wouldn't mind if Don Peppino stayed away for longer," said Etta. But as they entered the house, her smile died away. Unlike Dora, she didn't care for the stone floor, nor the wooden-beamed ceiling, nor the large living room with its ancient furniture, nor the pumpkins and decorations laid out on the heavy table with its marble top. No, all Etta noticed was that the place was chillingly cold, awfully musty and thoroughly inhospitable.

2
CLAIRVOYANT

In the gloomy living room stood a pale, skinny woman with ash-blonde hair and washed-out blue eyes bulging from her plain face. With a mousy voice, she welcomed them.

"Silvana is our neighbour," Benedetta explained. "She's a permanent resident of Col di Favilla who's been helping us with the party preparations."

"Isn't it lonely when the temporary residents leave?" Dora asked Silvana.

"It is and it isn't. The forest is full of kindred spirits, many of whom have lived all their life in Col di Favilla, and some of whom I have known all my life. Mr and Mrs Puppa have moved here permanently, as has Ugo ..."

"I'm not sure he counts as a kindred spirit," said Etta.

"We met him by the church," Benedetta explained, "and he had one of his outbursts. He can be so silly at times."

A shiver sailed over Silvana's skinny body. "Anger is never a good thing," she murmured, as if to herself.

"Who's angry? Not Ugo *again*?" Etta immediately recognised the deep voice as belonging to the woman she'd spoken to on the phone. Mrs Adele Strikeheaven wasn't tall, but she had an imposing energy about her that seemed to double her size. By contrast, Silvana dwindled even further into the background.

"Yes, Ugo again, I'm afraid," said Benedetta. "He's hopeless, but he won't spoil our party."

"Of course he won't," said Adele. As the introductions were made, Etta looked at her host and realised how ugly the woman was. Maybe it was the huge nose or the small eyes under bushy brows; maybe the irregular shape of her face. "But before anything else," Adele continued, unaware of Etta's observations, "our guests need a hot shower."

To Etta's horror, the bedroom she, Dora and Leon were shown to was even chillier than the living room. The shower, while not cold, wasn't as hot as she would have wished, and the bathroom was draughty. Dora, of course, was oblivious to these issues. She simply wanted to return to the others and help with the preparations for the party. At least Leon looked equally concerned.

"Let's go," conceded Etta. "After all, the only comfortable place in this bedroom would be under the blankets."

On their return, a fire had been lit in the living room's large fireplace. Enormously pleased, Leon sat down where the ancient terracotta tiles were warm, Dora glad that a fire screen would protect him from roasting like a chestnut.

While Dora made garlands, cooked candied apples and prepared a variety of scary finger foods, Etta tried to help. But after a few failed attempts, she was politely invited to sit down before she did more harm than good. Easily bored, she stopped next to a framed picture almost hidden behind a lamp in the living room. It was of two young women, one extremely pretty and the other extremely ugly. The pretty one was almost identical to Benedetta.

"That's Mum and Auntie Adele," Benedetta explained, "when they were about the same age I am now."

"Where was this taken?"

1. A Tuscan Threat

"In Fiesole," Adele replied.

"You don't look like you were having much fun," Etta said.

"I've never been that photogenic. I always look like Miss Contrary."

"Same here," murmured Etta sympathetically.

FOR DINNER, SILVANA PREPARED RIBOLLITA, A TYPICALLY TUSCAN minestrone soup made with Tuscan kale, beans, veggies and stale bread. As usual, Dora was eager to learn the recipe. Thinking she was helping, she picked up some dried leaves that she thought were marjoram and went to throw them into the mix.

"Not those," Adele stopped her. "They're St John's Wort."

"Oh, I'm so sorry," Dora said, bringing them to her nose.

"Don't worry." Adele indicated the next jar. "Those are valerian roots; the bitterness would have ruined the ribollita. I use them to prepare a herbal tea, as I do have trouble sleeping."

"Adele's tea works wonders on me, too," said Silvana. "Now I sleep, but unfortunately, I keep having such bad dreams…"

"You're too sensitive." Benedetta went on to explain further as she led Etta and Dora from the kitchen to the living room. "Silvana has the Gift, even if she doesn't look like…"

"The Gift?"

"She's clairvoyant."

"Like Cassandra in Castelmezzano," Dora said. "She's the local witch."

"Our Silvana is more than a witch," Benedetta said. "She seems to be able to see things from the past as well as possible futures."

"Nonsense!" Etta exclaimed. She didn't believe in clairvoyance, or witches.

Benedetta laughed. "Most likely so, but still, it's good to have her about. She will be doing tarot readings for our guests tomorrow."

"Did you mention the tarot?" Adele asked as she and Silvana joined the three women in the living room.

"Yes, I was telling Etta and Dora about tomorrow."

"I don't think I can do it," Silvana protested.

"Of course you can."

"But, I've never…"

"Just make it up," Benedetta explained. "Say something about a past love or suffering, and then promise future happiness."

"But I've never used the cards for that…"

"It's just pretend, and the guests will know that."

"She needs some practice," Adele said firmly. "Take those cards out. She will feel more confident tomorrow then."

"I'd love to know what's in store for me," Dora said.

AFTER DINNER, SILVANA TOOK THE CARDS AND ASKED DORA TO CUT the deck. She then dealt out five cards face down in the shape of a cross and turned over the one on the left.

"There was an important man in your past. But this is the King of Spades, who is a flawed character…"

"My poor dear father had a gambling addiction," Dora sighed.

"In your present, I see the Angel of Temperance, pouring water into wine. You're the peacemaker, bringing patience and moderation, but these next cards don't tell me much more," Silvana said, turning the two cards above and below the central one. "As for the future, there's the Chariot, a dynamic symbol for movement and transformation."

"That'll be our trusty Fiat 500," said Dora and they all laughed.

1. A Tuscan Threat

"You see, Silvana, it wasn't too bad at all," said Adele encouragingly.

"I'll be next," cried Benedetta eagerly, reaching out to cut the deck.

"First, let me serve Silvana's herbal tea so she gets some sleep tonight," interrupted Adele, suddenly seeming less anxious to see her friend in action. As she poured the tea into a mug, her hand trembled a bit and a splash ended up on the cards. Adele quickly wiped them with the cloth she had used to hold the teapot.

Dora smelled the air. "It doesn't stink too badly for something made with valerian root." However, she declined a share in Silvana's drink, while Etta made her feelings clear by wrinkling her nose. Silvana took a sip, clearly not taking much pleasure from the taste, but smiling nonetheless.

"I've had so many restless nights recently, filled with nightmares. Silly me!"

"Oh, come on," Benedetta said. "Tell me if I will finally find the man of my dreams."

Silvana laid out the cards in formation again and turned the one on the left.

"The wheel of fortune," she said. "I guess it refers to you having had two wonderful parents and a happy childhood, but all things must come to an end. And life goes on."

A sudden shadow fell over Benedetta's sparkling eyes. "That's the trouble with having your cards read by someone who knows you," she said quietly. Silvana shrugged, her hand going to the card above the one in the centre of the cross.

"The Hermit," read Etta, her green eyes devouring the picture. Totally sceptical, she was also curious as a cat.

"And he's head down!" said Dora.

"Is that a good sign?" asked Benedetta.

"A card head down tends to have a negative meaning. So a hermit could be a sign of peace or mindfulness, but head down…" Silvana tapped the central card. "Of course, it depends on what's here."

"I'm sure," said the always optimistic Dora, "we'll find something nice for your present and future. That hermit of yours might simply be in a bad mood."

"If he's who I'm thinking of, I doubt it's temporary," Etta couldn't resist airing her opinion. Dora sent her what was meant to be a nasty glare, but Etta hardly noticed.

Silvana turned the next card. Suddenly, the playful chitchat died into tense silence.

Leaning against its sharp scythe was the Grim Reaper.

"Now, that's something!" exclaimed Benedetta, startled. "I can't see the point in looking at the other cards after the Reaper." Benedetta had meant her words light heartedly, but poor Silvana was trembling from head to toe, her already fragile figure crumpling like a fallen leaf.

"Don't look so terrified, this is just a joke," Adele said as imperiously as she could, but Etta had the impression she was more disturbed than she cared to show. "Please, Benedetta, take those cards away. We will do without tarot readings tomorrow. We still have to bake a few trays of witches' fingers. When the last set is in the oven, we can carve more pumpkins. Etta, I'd be grateful if you would wash the pumpkins so Benedetta and I can decorate them later. Just cut their tops off and clear out the seeds."

In the short time since they had met, it seemed Adele had already got the measure of Etta's limited artistic talents.

3
A SENSE OF FOREBODING

"I knew it! I told Adele I shouldn't touch those tarot cards," whispered Silvana as Dora and Leon accompanied her home. "Every time I get close to the Other World – it doesn't matter if it's for real or just a joke – something happens. The spirits want to speak to me."

"Has it always been like that?" Dora asked.

"Since I was a child, but only my grandmother could understand what was going on."

"You don't really think something bad is gonna happen to Benedetta, do you? She's such a bright, happy soul."

"Oh, I wish I knew for certain, but truth is, I'm worried. I have been for weeks."

"The spirits have been alerting you for that long?"

"Not directly, but I feel something wicked and evil at work. And yes, I'm really afraid for Benedetta."

"But the Halloween party is going to be fun with people there you've known for ages. Why would anyone want to harm such a lovely young woman?"

"Madness. A streak of madness, of fury has been growing day by day…"

"Maybe you're just too sensitive to human emotions. Luckily, most of us don't go around harming people; we have the ability to resist our baser instincts. But just in case, we can keep our eyes open thanks to your warning."

By the time Dora and Leon returned to the mill, Benedetta had gone to bed. Adele left the pumpkin she was carving and invited Dora and Etta to sit with her.

"So, what do you think?"

"Think about what?"

Adele fixed her eyes on Etta, a thin smile appearing on her face.

"I appreciate that you want to keep a cool mind and avoid romanticising the whole thing. I've wondered myself if I'm letting my imagination run wild, influenced by this place and the fact we're here all by ourselves. Up until now, we've always visited in the summer when there's more people around."

"How long have you been here this time? And has something else happened, apart from the tarot reading?"

"We arrived three weeks ago, after a good month in Florence at Benedetta's. These old houses, even if thoroughly modernised..." Etta's brows rose to her hairline; there was nothing modern about the mill, with its cold water and draughty rooms, but with a great effort, she kept her sarcasm to herself "... need time and care to run smoothly. The first few days were OK, but then Silvana started with her visions and Benedetta's mood became sombre, which is unlike her. Even with Piero and Francesca Puppa here, the atmosphere has started to feel heavy and oppressive, as if we are all trying too hard to be light hearted, despite feeling that something is wrong – very wrong. Then it all came to a head today with those silly tarot cards! But they can't mean anything, can they? They're just a party trick, an illusion…"

Etta shook her head. "Why did you call us in?"

For the first time, Adele Strikeheaven seemed uncertain. "I'm good friends with the Italian President of the Home Swapping Circle. She lives in Tuscany, not too far from here. She mentioned that two of her members – and their dog, of course – had been travelling around Germany, helping the police solve crimes. I couldn't call the police on the back of a feeling of foreboding, but I thought if you were to visit, you could maybe prevent the feeling becoming reality. If I'm wrong and everything is fine, you will still have visited our charming part of Tuscany, which most tourists miss…"

Etta closed her eyes like a cat indulging in something pleasurable. Deep in thought, she sat still for a long while. When she finally opened her eyes again, she saw Dora nodding as if to tell Adele that this was good: a reassuring sign that Etta was putting her precious grey cells to work.

"I need more backstory," Etta said.

"Backstory?"

"Yes, Adele, tell me about Benedetta. What happened to her parents? What's your role in her life? How long has it been so? That kind of backstory."

"It's a simple, if rather sad story," said Adele, her face displaying more emotion than usual. "My sister – a beautiful woman – and her husband died in a hiking accident in the Alps in the spring, and I came over to Florence to care for Benedetta. She has no family on her father's side, and on her mother's, there's just me…"

"How come you and your sister ended up in Tuscany?"

"My sister and I came from the US to study art in Florence, and both married Italian men. But I was unlucky enough to lose my husband two years after our wedding. He came from Col di Favilla and is buried in the Isola Santa graveyard, where you started your hike. After his death, I hung around Italy for a while, then decided to settle in Columbus, Ohio. I return to my house here in Tuscany whenever I have a chance..."

"And your sister?"

"She stayed in Italy with her husband and their daughter. Whenever I came over from the States, I'd visit them in Florence before coming back here."

"Who restored the mill?"

"My husband, of course. Why do you ask?"

"Just curious. He must have loved the place."

"He did. When we first met, he lived in Pisa, but we put aside a little each month so we could keep the mill..."

"You must have been very fond of your husband," Dora butted in. "Other wives would have sold this property – its maintenance must be a nightmare."

"It is, but I would feel like I'm betraying his memory if I were to sell this place or allow it to decay."

"Has anything happened over the summer?" asked Etta. "Anything unusual, I mean. Did Benedetta stay with you here?"

"Of course my niece came to stay here. There were lots of things to take care of – Italian laws are bizarre to say the least, and we had to make sure our accountant found a way to bypass as much inheritance tax as possible. Tax men everywhere are ready to help themselves, even taking from Benedetta who's too young to have worked for a living..."

"Forgive the impertinence of this question: is her inheritance a large one?"

"My brother-in-law was a rich man, so yes, Benedetta has inherited a fortune. But I can't see what that has to do with what's happening here in Col di Favilla. She's got no connection with this place, except through me..."

"I just want to look at the whole picture. So, she came to Col di Favilla this summer?"

"For the first time in years, yes."

1. A Tuscan Threat

"And did either of you notice anything strange?"

Adele added some logs to the fire. "They will keep the house warm till the morning." Again, Etta kept a somewhat different opinion to herself. "Actually, it was a good summer. Plenty of people came over, many of whom you will meet tomorrow. It was good for Benedetta to get a change of scenery; to start with, she had mentioned going back to Florence after a couple of weeks, but in the end, she only returned to sort out paperwork. She was content here."

"Why?"

Adele looked at Etta blankly. "What do you mean, why? She was away from painful memories. She had my support, nice people to chat to, events to attend in Isola Santa and the neighbouring villages. It was as good a summer as possible after suffering such a tremendous loss."

"Oh, come on! A girl who lives in Florence, happy here among elderly people? Perhaps for a week or two, but months? There must have been some reason, something – or someone – that attracted her interest."

"You're astute, Etta Passolina. I can tell you're one of those people we can't hide anything from. I didn't want to put ideas into your head, to influence you, but since you asked… during the summer, Benedetta got close to that man, Ugo Ugolotto."

"How close?"

"Not very. I mean, something must have gone wrong as they stopped meeting, and in September, we returned to Florence for the whole month. And yes, I was relieved, if you must know. I don't like that man, although I might be biased by my affection for my niece. Apart from that, I cannot think of anything else."

"Do you think he might have been courting your niece because of her money?"

"Don't you? He's barely got enough to cover his needs, so what a stroke of luck when a girl arrives who stands to inherit a fortune. Unfortunately for him, things didn't turn out as he wished."

"Might he be out for revenge?"

Adele took her time before answering. "It would be unfair of me to suspect him of something that evil. But it seems your thinking is aligned to mine, despite my attempts not to influence you. Let's hope that by tomorrow evening, we can look back on this conversation and laugh."

"Let's hope so."

On climbing into bed, Etta was grateful that Dora had had the foresight to warm up a couple of hot water bottles earlier and place them between the sheets. The room was icy, but in her cosy cocoon, sleep caught her instantly.

4

A DEADLY NEIGHBOUR

The next morning, Etta woke up feeling unexpectedly warm. In fact, she was sweating under the blankets, her bladder compressed as if a dead weight was pressing her down into the mattress. Only when she was fully awake did she realise it was Leon. Dora must have pulled him up on to the bed during the night – somewhere he only slept when his fear of thunder or fireworks overcame his sense of dignity.

"It's you, my hushpuppy," Etta said, tickling the long body. Leon stretched, uttering incoherent guttural sounds as he rubbed his face and body against the fleece. He could never resist his bipeds tickling him.

"You're such an irresistible fellow," Etta said, smacking him affectionately on the head as Dora woke up. Etta immediately felt embarrassed; she preferred to keep her feelings hidden. After 60 years of referring to dogs as hairy, smelly, all-peeing creatures, she could still hardly believe she shared a roof with one, let alone a bed. Of course, she knew that Dora knew she loved the dog immensely, but there was a mutual understanding that Etta's *weakness* would never be mentioned.

"There was a storm last night," Dora said simply, keeping her side of the bargain.

"You did the right thing letting the dog join us, then," Etta replied crisply. "I was so tired, I must have slept through it." The two women had both been exhausted, so they hadn't even discussed the day's events before falling into a deep sleep. Now, Dora decided it was time to catch up.

"What do you think of last night?"

"I don't really know. If it had just been about Silvana and her stupid cards, I wouldn't be worried at all. She's scared of her own shadow anyway, but seeing someone as strong as Adele on edge… that's what's scared me."

"Maybe Silvana's fear has rubbed off on her…"

"No chance! A strong-willed woman like Adele won't be influenced that easily. We need to keep our eyes and ears open."

In the kitchen, Benedetta and her aunt were already hard at work, along with the timid Silvana and a woman Etta and Dora didn't recognise.

"You should have given us a shout and we would have got up earlier!" Dora was always ready to help out with the cooking and crafting, and she loved to be involved in the chitchat.

"You looked so tired, it was good you had a long rest," said Adele. "This is Mrs Puppa…"

"Please, call me Francesca," said the woman, smiling at the newcomers.

"Francesca has baked a chestnut cake that you can enjoy with your latte. And I've got some American bacon for Leon."

The hound jumped up, his ears pricked. After yesterday's stale bread, today was going to be different.

Etta insisted on having breakfast in the busy kitchen. "It's nice and warm with the oven on," she said with her usual lack of tact.

"I hope you haven't been too cold," Benedetta said.

1. A Tuscan Threat

"Oh no, we've been comfy," lied Dora, at the same moment as Etta said, "A little", silently adding *too much*.

"We're planning to do some modernisation. Next Halloween, you won't find the mill damp or draughty."

"Silly girl," said Adele to her niece. "There're more important things to do with your money. Now, please take a look at those madeleines in the oven. I'm not sure how you're going to decorate them to look like eyeballs."

Benedetta laughed. "I'll show you. The children will adore them."

As Dora put on an apron and prepared to help, Etta felt like a fish out of water.

"I'll take Leon for his walk," she said. "It seems dry outside."

"It's going to be a beautiful day," said Silvana, adding gloomily, "At least, if the forecast is to be believed."

"Silvana, please!" Adele reproached her.

"Etta, just be careful," Dora said from the table, her rolling pin already in action. "When I went out with Leon last night, I noticed some Dog's Lugs…"

"*Dog's Lugs*?" cried Etta, horrified.

"It's another name for Foxgloves," said Francesca. "Adele's neighbour has a bed of them behind his roses. They're not in flower now, so how did you spot them, Dora?"

"Leon wanted to pee, so I lit my torch and there they were."

"If he merely pees on them, he'll be fine," Adele said, grinning mischievously.

"Oh no, that won't do," said Dora, just in case Etta took Adele's words seriously.

LEON LOVED COL DI FAVILLA. THE SMELL OF WILD ANIMALS surrounded the houses, the day was sunny and fresh, the place was mysterious, and he looked forward to a good adventure after the quietness of his adoptive village of Castelmezzano down south, where he lived with his two bipeds. Etta was having a hard time following him as he disappeared into the vegetation, hunting for hare, squirrel or roe deer. It was useless calling him back; the stubborn dog did what he pleased, when he pleased.

"At least catch a wild boar, something we can all eat," she harrumphed, finally placing Leon on his leash. Wearing his most obedient expression, he turned doleful eyes on her, wondering why she would use such brutal methods to stop a poor hound from doing his job. He followed her, mortified by the injustice of life.

When they were almost home, Leon stopped in front of the neighbour's house. Etta pulled him gently, but the dog did not budge a millimetre. As Etta pulled harder, he decided it was time to use his superpower. He sat. And when Leon sat, he was no longer a common hound; instead, his weight would multiply, his 30 kilogrammes becoming as heavy and unmovable as the large stack of firewood behind their hosts' house.

For her part, Etta had learned to acknowledge when the battle was lost. She stopped, looked over the low stone wall behind some flowerless rosebushes and recognised Ugo Ugolotto.

"Good morning," she said, uncertain how the brusque man would respond. "It seems my dog wants to say hi…"

The man had his hands deep in the soil of a flowerbed. Dora would have recognised the tall yellow flowers, but Etta could barely distinguish a daisy from a poppy.

"Let him come."

Etta unleashed the dog, who ran to the man, sat down in front of him and tilted his head, his expression typically languid. Even the grumpiest person would have found him hard to resist, and Ugo scratched the hound's head. As Leon rose to his feet, the man vigorously massaged his body. The dog loved it.

"Are those flowers Foxgloves?" Etta asked. The man looked startled, but if he was shocked by her ignorance, he hid it well.

"The Foxgloves are in front of you, behind the roses. These are Jerusalem artichokes. This year has been so mild, a few are still flowering, but I have harvested some," and he showed her the misshapen tubers.

"Why?"

"They are delicious."

"Never heard of them."

"You'll get to try some this evening." He removed dirt from one tuber and passed it to Etta. "I'll be taking a few Jerusalem artichoke croquettes to the party…"

"You're coming to the party?" Etta's eyebrows shot up well above her large glasses.

"Maybe I've been too uncooperative, so I want to apologise to Benedetta. After all, it's not her fault she has an aunt like that…"

"I wouldn't say that when you hand over your gift," said Etta, all of a sudden wise to the sensitivities of others. "What made you change your mind?"

"Your friend."

"You mean Dora?" Etta handed the tuber back, trying to look impressed.

"She was here twenty minutes or so ago. She said she needed a break, too many cooks in the kitchen…"

"And?"

"Well, she said she understood my wish to escape from the rat race in Milan and search for the real meaning of life…"

"She encouraged you?"

"Not exactly. She warned me to make sure I don't fall from the rat race into the comfy trap."

"The comfy trap?" Etta repeated, confused. Where had her friend been leading this strange conversation?

"I didn't know what she meant either, so she explained.

When everything in our life runs smoothly and we feel comfortable all the time…"

"Sounds like heaven!" interrupted Etta.

"But when every day is the same, predictable, we end up taking no risk whatsoever and miss opportunities to learn new things. She mentioned that you've taken many risks together, sharing a house and expenses so that you could travel, and ever since, your life has been full of surprises, new people and good friendships."

"She told you all that?"

"And more. She said that in December, you're driving all the way to a Danish island in your Fiat 500. You're both well over 60, but the world is opening up to you."

"Maybe she's exaggerating a bit," Etta replied, but the sparkle in her eyes told a different story.

"But with her comfy trap, she described exactly how I've been feeling this past year. I'm ostensibly living my perfect life, but a part of me yearns for a good challenge, and now your friend has opened my eyes. I don't need to meet people because I'm lonely, but so I can learn more about the world and myself…"

"I guess 'people' includes Benedetta?"

The man flushed, becoming as red as the leaves of the maple tree behind him.

"We could do things together," he stammered hoarsely. "She loves it here too…"

5

HALLOWEEN!

When demons howl and shriek unseen,
And fears burst forth from night's dark screen,
It's just another Halloween...

BY LATE AFTERNOON, THE GUESTS WERE STARTING TO ARRIVE. Mostly from Florence or other Tuscan towns, they planned to stay in their Col di Favilla houses for the weekend as Halloween had fallen on a Friday. People from neighbouring villages were also happy to join in the spooky celebrations, and the children certainly looked the part in their terrifying costumes.

Benedetta had organised the games. Along with the traditional apple bobbing, there was to be a team competition to see who could find the most giant plastic spiders and bats hidden around the village and forest. There would be extra points for the team that returned with the tarantula! As for the adults, the villagers had brought small handicrafts to sell. And, of course, there was plenty of delicious food and drink on offer. Even Don Mangione, the local Priest, agreed that the Lord's ways could be rather mysterious. He could turn a blind eye to the children dressed up as witches and ghouls and the carved pumpkins lit from the inside by flickering candles, but for the safety of his parishioners, he'd better check the food.

When the sun went down, the buffet began. Etta would never be able to explain what caught her eye in the stampede of hungry guests, but her attention focused on a woman with a large tray, walking from the house and heading straight to Benedetta, who selected one of the items on offer.

"Wait!" cried Etta as the young woman bit into it.

"What?" Benedetta almost choked, gulping down the food to make room for air to reach her lungs.

"What are you eating?"

"They're croquettes, from Ugo," the woman with the tray explained.

"Why did you offer them to Benedetta first?"

"Because he told me they were especially for her."

"Did he ask you to give her one in particular?" Both women looked at Etta as if she were a lunatic. "I'm serious," Etta growled in her I'm-a-teacher-you'd-better-answer tone of voice. "Did he select one for her?"

"No, of course not," the woman replied, looking like a seven-year-old facing her strictest school mistress, "they're all the same."

Etta turned to Benedetta. "Are you feeling OK?" She grabbed the rest of the croquette from the young woman's hands, smelling it. It seemed fine, but it could contain an odourless poison.

"Yes, of course I'm OK. They're good."

Etta took a little bite, and yes, the croquette was good. Could a man poison a whole village just because one woman had spurned him? Neither Silvana nor the tarot cards had mentioned mass murder. Still, there was something disturbing Etta.

Am I letting Silvana influence me? No chance! I'm as strong willed as Adele. Still...

Leaving Benedetta looking gobsmacked, Etta went into the kitchen where the cooks, including Dora, were working full speed to replenish the buffet.

"What's this?" She pointed to two large pots on the cooker. Cinnamon sticks, star anise and apples pierced with cloves were floating in the liquid they contained.

"Mulled cider," Francesca Puppa answered from behind her. "You will love it." The liquid from one pan was being served into real glasses, the other into plastic cups. "The cups are for the children. That pan contains a non-alcoholic apple juice spiced up and carbonated."

"What else does the grown-up one contain?"

"A large glug of rum," Francesca winked at her, "to warm us up for the evening."

To feel warm in this house, I'd have to become an alcoholic, thought Etta, but once more, she was tactful enough to keep silent. Dora would surely be impressed.

"Is the tray of children's drinks ready?" asked Adele from the other side of the kitchen.

"Just sending it out now."

"Remember to pour one for Benedetta, she's teetotal."

"Done," said Francesca, filling the plastic mug Adele handed to her and placing it amongst the glasses.

Dora glanced at the tray critically. "Wouldn't it be better to put Benedetta's drink in a real glass? Its reddish colour will make it stand out from the others, but then she will be able to join in the glass clinking."

"Just make sure she gets the right one," Francesca said. "She can't even stand the smell of alcohol."

Dora nodded and did as she had suggested, removing the plastic cup and replacing it with a glass of non-alcoholic apple juice.

"Now," said Adele with her usual vigour, "let's see what's going on before we take out the grown-up glasses. I want the table to be cleared of all food so we can get started with the cakes and biscuits."

The kitchen emptied as the cooks invited the willing guests to finish the few things left on the buffet. Then they returned in good humour to prepare the grand finale of cakes and cider. They moved all the desserts into position, and Francesca followed with the large tray of drinks, the glasses clinking against one another.

Etta had her eyes fixed on Adele. Lost in thought, the woman didn't seem to notice. Then her eyes opened in horror and she sped after Francesca. And Etta was right behind her.

"Stop right there!" Adele cried. Startled, Francesca turned to look at her.

"Have I done something wrong?"

"No, not at all. It's just... I'm tired and thirsty. I think I'll take Benedetta's glass." Her trembling hand flew over the tray until it located the reddish drink. When she picked it up, she was shaking so hard, she had to steady one hand with the other.

"Is everything OK?" Francesca asked, flabbergasted.

"Of course. Tell Benedetta to take a cup from the children's tray."

Adele turned to find Etta glaring at her. She brought the glass to her lips.

"I wouldn't," Etta said smoothly. Adele stared back defiantly as she emptied the entire glass in a single gulp, then stalked into the kitchen.

Etta followed, picking up a gardener's glove from the floor.

"Did you drop this?" she asked, sitting in front of Adele, startling the other woman. "This is Ugo's, isn't it?"

"It is."

"What a clever way to frame him."

"I didn't frame anyone..."

"That's because you changed your plans at the last moment."

The woman lowered her head. "Yes."

"Why make the plans in the first place? Hard feelings, by any chance?"

"What?"

"Between you and your sister, who was such a *beautiful* woman."

Adele clutched at her throat as if she were suffocating.

"Some secrets are better shared and put into perspective. If you dwell on them alone, they mutate into greater horrors than any we've seen this Halloween."

Adele shrugged. "I guess I've got nothing to lose now. Yes, I hated my sister – my *beautiful* sister. It was bad enough that I was the ugly duckling, but she would poke fun at my looks with our relatives, our friends. When I got married, I thought I was finally free of her. I experienced joy and happiness for the first time, but then, my husband died, while she married a rich man and had a child with him. Her life was perfect.

"Even then, though, I wouldn't have minded if it hadn't been for her continuing to call me an ugly failure whenever our paths crossed. Then the accident took this beautiful woman with her ugly soul. I decided I'd leave Social Services to take care of Benedetta, but then I thought again. I could never love her – my sister hurt me too deeply for me to forgive …"

"So when you realised her interest in Ugo was getting serious, you had no qualms about planning to kill her."

"As long as Benedetta didn't marry, I would have the money I needed to restore Mosceta Mill. It's here that my husband left his heart. I love this place so much – beyond reason – that I was ready to kill my niece and frame that stupid man."

"You know what a strong influence you have on Silvana, so she became your unwitting ally. You just had to hint at bad omens, drop in a few words about the threat of Ugo's aggression, and she'd do the rest by believing they were her feelings, her sensations, her premonitions. Then it was time for the old trick of spilling a drink over the cards, giving you the opportunity to place the Grim Reaper on top of the pack..."

"Yes, I planned it all," Adele admitted quietly.

"And that included mixing St John's Wort as well as valerian into Silvana's herbal tea to make it more likely she'd experience nightmares. This is why her tea didn't smell as bitter as it would if it had merely contained valerian."

Adele nodded.

"When the President of the Home Swapping Circle mentioned my reputation as an amateur sleuth..."

"I believed you were really just an old lady who'd solved those crimes through luck, not judgement, but your reputation would add credibility to my worries and Silvana's premonitions."

"Finally, you dropped Foxglove in Benedetta's glass while the others were busy clearing the buffet, and made sure we'd find something belonging to Ugo. After all, the Foxglove had grown in his garden."

"Are you the Devil?" Adele pressed her hands against her bosom, sweat beading her face.

"More like your Guardian Angel. I tipped away the contents of Benedetta's glass and filled another from the children's pan."

It took a few seconds for Adele to understand the implication of Etta's words.

"I didn't drink any poison?"

"Just apple juice."

"How will I face Benedetta?" Adele looked towards the kitchen door, then back to Etta, her expression a mix of relief and despair.

"She doesn't need to know..."

"You trust me not to try to harm her again?"

"You're such a stubborn woman! Are you not aware of your feelings yet? You didn't kill your niece because you love her. And you love her because she's nothing like her awful mother."

1. A Tuscan Threat

Under her huge nose, Adele's mouth dropped in total amazement.

"Had you told people what a b... b... what a nasty sister you had, you would never have nurtured the monster inside yourself. You would have lived a much happier life."

All of a sudden, strong, iron-willed Adele Strikeheaven burst into tears. "My dear little girl..."

"Your dear little girl might end up marrying, but she won't forget about you, or the mill. Trust me." Etta patted the woman on the shoulder. "I've been there. I had a dreadful husband, but I felt too guilty to complain to anyone. Therefore, no one realised the real monster was the smiling, apparently friendly man, rather than his cranky wife."

Adele looked Etta in the eyes, seeing – possibly for the first time in her life – an understanding that went well beyond words.

"Thank you," she finally managed to mutter.

"What for? After all, it was you who called me to stop something wicked from happening." Etta looked at the empty glass beside Adele and winked at her. "A woman like you would be a great loss to the world."

As Adele cast her eyes to the ground, looking as if she were gathering up fragments of herself and her life that she'd never understood before, Etta noticed a subtle movement in her peripheral vision. Dora's head popped around the door, followed by a thumbs up. Then Etta remembered Dora insisting on changing Benedetta's cup for a glass. Had she known all along?

Leon, dozing under the kitchen table, awoke with a "Woof, woof, WOOF!" Disaster had been averted and peace restored; it was time for his humans to turn their attention to the essentials: a Basset Hound's dinner.

2. A CHRISTMAS MYSTERY IN VENICE

THE HOMESWAPPERS MYSTERIES - A SHORT STORY

1

CANAL GRANDE

It was wretchedly cold.

Like the Venetians, Concetta Natale Passolina, simply known as Etta to her friends, stayed inside the vaporetto, wrapped up in her scarf and woollen hat. Although she was aware that hats didn't suit her, they were the only weapon she had to defend against headaches and the army of other pains threatening a sexagenarian at the latter end of that particular decade. To someone like Etta, used to the dry mountain air of the Southern Apennines, this damp lagoon was an environment more suitable for fish and frogs than human beings. And from what her friend, Dorotea Rosa Pepe – or simply Dora, when Etta was in a good mood – had told her, they had a while to go yet: all the way down from the head to the tail of the long snake called the Grand Canal.

For some inexplicable reason, the door to the interior of the water bus kept on being left open by passengers and staff alike. Two of the top windows were jammed open – she had already unsuccessfully tried to close them, to funny looks from her fellow passengers, so she now sat in discomfort, wriggling to find the best position to cuddle up into herself and avoid most of the draughts of frigid air.

The vaporetto came to its third – or was it the fourth? – stop, but Dora didn't give any indication from outside that they were about to arrive at their destination. Dora's body was supporting itself against the boat's railing as her hands were too busy clasping each other in adoration. Her head was turning left to right, right to left; her mouth was wide open in wonder. An incredulous smile had spread across her upper and lower – much lower than normal – lip. Her peppery fringe had lengthened in the damp air, reaching down to cover her eyebrows. From time to time, one hand would leave the embrace of the other to push her hair out of her eyes.

Sitting beside Dora was a proud Basset Hound. He was evidently busy taking in all the new smells, but his demeanour showed he was only too well aware of how many human eyes were resting on him in admiration. Napoleon – his noble name often shortened to Leon, much to the dog's dismay – never thought anyone would find him amusing or silly. As Etta had often found out to her cost, the stubborn dog had rather a high opinion of himself and liked things his own way.

Stop number four – or was it five? – came and went, but Dora still showed no sign of moving. Either it was raining, or it was so damp, it might as well have been. Etta could see the green cloak Dora was wearing getting darker and darker with moisture, her fringe longer and longer.

It was time to bring the woman back to Planet Earth. Etta sighed so loudly, the passenger sitting beside her started and looked at her as if fearing she might not be well. Etta raised her palms to the sky and pointed to Dora with her nose, mutely attempting to explain to a perfect stranger the cause of such a big exhale.

Etta stood, her legs unstable beneath her. A vaporetto makes one as seasick as any other small vessel hitting the choppy ocean

2. A Christmas Mystery in Venice

waters. And a Venetian canal is prone to the same rolling waves as anywhere else on the Mediterranean. Bravely, she managed to stagger outside and touch Dora on the arm as the woman was staring straight ahead, mesmerised.

"Isn't this wonderful? I'm so glad you decided to come out..." and Dora pointed to the infinite succession of houses that surrounded the Grand Canal, their lights already on. The sky was dark blue in the immediate afterglow of the sunset, but still light enough to hint at the bright reds, oranges and pinks of the buildings' façades and their intricate decorations, as if they were the work of a keen knitter. The gondolas were tied and rolling in front of jetties dotted with colourful striped poles, the yellow lamplights illuminating their slim shapes in the incoming darkness and reflecting them on the wet pavements.

"The Rialto Bridge!" cried Dora, almost choking in her total bliss.

The bright white structure crossing the canal shone, capturing any light left in the cloudy sky. Its 13 arches, adorned with Christmas lights, oozed with romanticism; the dark passage under the bridge exuded mystery. A black gondola, its lamp lit, cut across the waters in front of them to leave room for the vaporetto...

Before she knew what she was doing, Etta was clasping her hands, opening and closing her mouth like a fish out of water. Standing beside Dora, she completely forgot to raise her hood over her hat, tighten her scarf, call her two companions inside...

"Biennale Gardens! This is us," said Dora a good 50 minutes after they had clambered on board the vaporetto.

"Wha-wha-what?" cried Etta. She hadn't understood a single word – had her companion spoken in ancient Aramaic? She was chilled to the bone, but she didn't even realise that.

41

"We've arrived, this is our stop. You left your luggage trolley inside – you'd better fetch it now. Or should I do it for you?"

"I can fetch my own trolley," snapped Etta, wondering how she could have left her luggage unattended for so long. *Most likely the fault of those narrow alleys – are they called calli? –with their ceilings of Christmas lights, St Mark's Square materialising in all its amazing grandeur, the huge Christmas tree beside the Doge Palace... and all the other wonders.*

By the time Etta came back on deck, the vaporetto staff had already opened the gate and were shouting the name of the pier stop: "Biennale Gardens." The two women and one dog walked onto the jetty and were finally on firm ground – what a reassuring feeling.

On Venice's mainland, a woman came towards them, a smile shining from beneath a thick layers of scarves.

"I'm guessing that's Leon, and you must be Etta and Dora."

"Giustina?" cried Dora, half asking, half stating as if meeting an old friend.

"That's me."

Dora introduced herself and her friend to make it clear which one was which.

"How come you took the Number 1?" the woman asked, nodding towards the departing vaporetto. "The number 5.1 or 6 would have got you here in twenty minutes without all those stops..."

Etta's eyes pierced Dora, who was the trip organiser. Dora always did plenty of research before their holidays and hardly ever made a mistake... not unwittingly, at least.

"I know," admitted Dora between an embarrassed cackle and a guilty expression, "but we wanted to arrive slowly. It's our first time on the Grand Canal, and we needed to have time to let it all sink in."

Giustina smiled. Etta gasped. Leon sighed.

"Please, follow me. Then you can get warm and snug in

2. A Christmas Mystery in Venice

Annamaria's flat – it's small, but cosy, and just a few metres away from me in Calle delle Ancore. But tell me more about this home swapping thing; Annamaria tried to explain, but I'm rather slow on the uptake."

Etta needed more time to recover from all the new sensations, and the cold that had attacked her on the boat, before she attempted to describe the 'homeswapping thing', which she found hard to explain at the best of times. But Dora had no such problem. She launched into the whole tale of how she and Etta had met after discovering the meagre figure the Italian Government was offering them as a pension in thanks for more than 40 – forty! – years of hard work as teachers. Feeling frustrated at the prospect of being virtual paupers, they had decided to share a house to cut down on the cost of living, and had then embraced homeswapping as a way of travelling not only cheaply, but...

"Deeply!" insisted Dora with passion, her damp fringe jumping around as her demeanour matched the enthusiasm in her voice. "You see, when you home swap, you not only live like a local, but you get to know people, loads of people, gaining an insider's knowledge of a place and making friends all around Europe..."

Giustina had plenty of questions as she guided them from calle to corte and over the bridges in the weird labyrinth of land and water that is Venice.

"This is Calle delle Ancore," she said finally, pointing to a blue-and-white sign on the wall, its paint peeling. She stopped in front of a wooden door. "And this is your home for the duration of your stay. I live just two doors away with my daughter." She indicated a red door framed with white stones. They must have passed it unnoticed, too busy chatting. "Now, let me show you inside the building."

They entered a two-room apartment with a bedroom and a large kitchen-living room. A small Christmas tree on the windowsill protected a Murano glass Nativity scene. To Etta's surprise, the apartment was warm and pleasant inside. The table lights were switched on and a bowl of fresh fruit sat next to a loaf of bread on a wooden board. A pot stood on the red vintage cooker.

"A soup I made for you," Giustina explained. She opened the oven door after switching it on and checked something inside. Then she explained about the waste collection, heating system, water boiler and answered all the questions from the new occupants.

"Now the explanations are over," she announced a good ten minutes later, "let's have a little aperitivo before I leave you to rest."

Giustina checked in the fridge and took out a bottle of prosecco, serving them half a glass each. Then, she went back to the oven and took out a tray filled with what she called "Cicchetti Veneziani" – Venetian tapas, now warm and ready to eat.

The slightly crunchy deep-fried prawns and anchovies looked wonderful, delicate with the aroma of the sea that only the freshest fish has. Little slices of polenta with baccalà mantecato – creamed salt cod; squid skewers; open sandwiches with eggs and anchovies; tuna meatballs – the cicchetti Veneziani was a feast for the senses even before Etta and Dora had tasted it.

It didn't take long for the three women to resume their chat. When Giustina explained how her husband had scarpered when their daughter was just four, leaving his family for a new life in Vienna, it enabled Etta to engage in one of her favourite hobbies: denigrating men for being men and describing her numerous misadventures with her former husband. Leon protested, determined to defend the male sex, but in response, he received a couple of anchovies that Dora had cleaned for him. Then he decided he might as well let the cranky crone carry on.

Eventually, Giustina got up, kissed the two women on the cheeks and took her leave with a final few instructions.

"Call me if you need me. Annamaria has left you a file with a list of her favourite places to eat or enjoy a Spritz, along with her most loved walks on the less travelled routes."

Dora's eyes fell on the file. This was one treasure she particularly looked forward to in every home swap: the key to the hidden secrets of any locality.

AFTER A GENEROUS DINNER OF SOUP AND ANOTHER HALF GLASS OF prosecco each, Etta offered to do the dishes while Dora suggested she take Leon for his night-time walk.

"Just a little walk, Leon," Etta recommended, waving her yellow rubber gloves in admonition, "just time enough for a pee."

Outside, Leon, who needed a little grass to inspire him to do his business, pulled Dora all the way back to the Biennale Gardens, which were not too far from Annamaria's flat. Once there, though, of course he needed to explore every single corner so that each statue, tree, pillar or whatever other vertical structure he found there would carry a not-so-permanent sign of His Majesty's passage. Dora often wondered how a single dog, no matter how long, could contain such an abundant reserve of pee and dispense it in little spritzes here and there. Wagner, Oberdan, Verdi, and other not-so-identifiable marble busts all had to be saluted by the scrupulous Basset. He launched himself in every direction, taking all the small paths into the greenery as if it were a warm summer's night.

Dora, as ever, found it hard to resist his enthusiasm. When the wet branches stopped restricting her view, she was surprised to be facing a tall door. Well, maybe it wasn't exactly a door, just a sort of majestic marble arch, but it looked like the entrance to somewhere. Only, it opened up onto the water, framing yet another stunning view of a secondary canal, the houses beyond it glowing with rows of lit windows.

Dora didn't even have the time to clasp her hands before she realised a man was standing a few steps in front of them, admiring the very same arch. The cold wind dropped just enough that she could hear his words...

"When the Venetians are tired of the established authorities, they go to these three secret places and, opening the doors at the bottom of those courtyards, they go forever to beautiful places and other stories."

He stared some more, then he left, unaware of Dora and Leon's presence. But Dora could not pull her eyes away from the magic door. She was certain she had read that very quote somewhere, but where?

As she pondered and looked, looked and pondered, she gave the four-legged one ample time to pee and sniff to his heart's content.

2

ACQUA ALTA

It seemed to Etta they'd had the most interesting touristy day, and it had been sunny. They had discovered that in their neighbourhood – Sestiere Castello, as the Venetians called it – they could buy fish directly from the local fishermen; their greengrocer's shop was a gondola at the end of their calle; their minimarket was in front of a rather shabby-looking bakery and café in which was served the best pastries she'd ever tried.

Once they'd finished their early-morning shopping, they had walked Riva degli Schiavoni, all the way from Sestiere Castello to Sestiere St Mark, facing the island of St George with the gleaming white façade of its Palladian church. Among the wooden poles, rows and rows of sleek black gondolas, protected by blue covers, stood perfectly aligned and dancing to the rhythm of the waves. Then the Giudecca island tempted them to take the vaporetto on the waterway, despite Etta not being so fond of leaving terra firma.

They passed the Bridge of Sighs, which to Etta's surprise was nowhere near as romantic as the Rialto Bridge. When Dora explained it had no reason to be romantic as it had in olden days been the passage to dark ominous prison cells, and sometimes execution, Etta wasn't convinced. World renowned as it was, the Bridge of Sighs came nowhere near to deserving its global reputation.

They had alighted near the Doge's Palace, which Etta was satisfied to see was a miracle of artistry. Like many of Venice's buildings, it had appeared from a distance to be the work of a skilled knitter rather than a master craftsman using brick, marble and stone. And when they came face to face with St Mark's Basilica, from the bottom of the square as Dora had insisted on walking away from the church without turning their heads until they'd reached a spot where they could view the marvel in its entire glory, they both felt their hearts almost jump out of their mouths with amazement.

Were they still in Italy or somewhere in the Middle East, closer to Istanbul than Rome? If someone had asked for directions to Samarkand, Etta would have considered it a legitimate request. The magnificent linear perspective of the Procuratie and the 98 metre-tall geometrical red-brick bell tower created the perfect contrast to the five round cupolas of the fanciful Basilica. As they got closer, they enjoyed the intricate details of the façade: the marble, the statues, the columns, and mostly the lunettes of the portals adorned with golden mosaics, glittering in the sun.

The two women had decided they would take it in turns to visit the Basilica, the other staying with Leon. Etta's turn would be in the afternoon, so dog and biped had only to find a place to sit and rest while waiting for Dora. After a fleeting look at the prices on the menus, Etta had resolved not to take coffee in St Mark's square. A few calli away, she could get two pastries and two cappuccino for less than the cost of a single espresso where they were currently standing.

"What the heck?" she cried. "It's not as if they're going to serve it accompanied by golden sugar. We will wait for Dora here and do without refreshments."

2. A Christmas Mystery in Venice

Etta and Leon were now sitting on one of the unique benches in the square that were ready to be transformed into a walkway if the unusually high tide, or acqua alta as the Venetians called it, that sometimes occurred at this time of year were to take them by surprise. Moved by the melancholy expression of the hound and clearly mistaking the two of them for beggars, tourists soon began to stop and ask if they could leave a little offering for the cute doggie. Etta wondered if it wouldn't be worth spending the 15 euros for an espresso at the Caffè Florian, if just to save her injured pride.

For his part, Leon enjoyed the great success of his ethereal expression. In response to the cooing from the tourists, he made his face even longer, his brow even more furrowed, his eyes even more liquid. He couldn't understand why the stubborn biped dismissed his efforts by refusing to take any of the money that, to the best of his knowledge, could be converted into a good steak in any restaurant. His former owner, the late Watchman of Rothenburg, would certainly have praised his ingenuity. But then again, females are made of different stuff to males.

The two Moors on the white-and-blue watchtower opposite them chimed twelve, signalling lunchtime was getting closer; when on holiday, they tended to have lunch around one o'clock, a little earlier than back home. The trouble was that while the Moors were still chiming, Dora came out of the Basilica, her eyes full of wonder. As she was trying to put into words all the treasures she'd seen; how she'd dreamed of visiting Venice for her entire lifetime, but still, her expectations had been exceeded by the beauty of the city, Etta and Leon looked at each other in dismay. How would they convince this dreamy woman there are elemental needs like eating, drinking and taking a rest that should not be forgotten, even in the face of the most exquisite beauties and treasures of the world?

"Talking of practical things," Dora seemed to read their minds, "we're not too far from Calle Bragadin…"

"Calle Bragadin? Is that where we can get some speciality food? I thought we'd done our groceries shopping for the day."

"Not for the body, but we can get some food for the soul. There's a bookshop…"

"But we've passed plenty of bookshops close to home."

"I know, but this one is special."

Etta sighed in resignation. "How far away is it?"

Dora pulled out her map and showed Etta. In fact, it didn't look too far as the crow flies, but Etta's sharp eyes noticed there was a maze of alleys to walk along, canals to cross, calli and campi to traverse to get there. Could one navigate one's way around Venice as one could in any other town? Frankly, she doubted it. Still, once an idea had entered Dora's brain, it was too much like hard work to try to talk her out of it.

"Are you looking for *your* book?"

"Yes." Dora liked to collect an illustrated copy of *Pippi Longstocking* from every new place they visited.

Etta sighed again. Leon was disconcerted; he wanted food, but at the same time, he was happy not to have to go home just yet. Holidays meant spending more time outside, trying new food in new places, dragging the two women wherever he wanted to go and, if he was lucky, finding a pretty she-Basset to fall in love with for a lifetime… or maybe just five minutes.

"I guess the most direct route is this way, past the tower of the two Moors," said Dora confidently. Under the clock tower they went, finding themselves in a long calle called Merceria dell'Orologio. It was bustling with crowds, multiple lines of white Christmas lights suspended above their heads while all manner of decorations cheered them from the infinite row of shop windows.

They hadn't gone far before Dora stopped, her nose in the air, under a tall stone portal. Above it was a bas relief of an old woman holding a mortar. This was Giustina, Dora told her companions with a chuckle, thinking about their neighbour, who

2. A Christmas Mystery in Venice

had saved the Venetian Government from being overthrown by a group of rebel aristocrats. Upon hearing some noises in the street, she had looked out to see what was going on, suspecting some foul deed, and let go of her heavy mortar, which landed on the rebel leader's head. The rest of the conspirators, fearing they had been discovered by the authorities, ran away. So grateful was the Venetian Government, Giustina's rent wasn't ever increased, not only for the rest of her lifetime, but for all future generations of her family.

As they resumed their walk, Etta gave the bas relief of Giustina a nod of approval. As far as she was concerned, dropping them on the heads of the bad guys was a far better use for cooking implements than… well, cooking. Luckily, Dora was a marvel in the kitchen, as Etta could burn the simplest of dishes.

They hadn't gone far before even Dora, usually ever the optimist, discovered that there's no such thing as a direct route in Venice. You simply cross too many streets – I beg your pardon, calli – along with quays, brooks or canals. Also, bridges which, for some obscure reason, have a tendency to move you away from your final destination. If you top it all with the many enchanting views at which you simply can't help stopping, or worse making a little deviation to take a photo, you shouldn't be surprised when you discover you've lost your way.

Needless to say, mobile phones are near to useless. Even if they know where your final destination is, they only have an approximate idea of where you are right now, and less idea where you're heading as you walk. The outcome tends to be your phone urging you to change direction every twenty steps or so. Compounding these troubles is the fact that there's no one you can really ask for directions – the only other people in the streets are fellow tourists, pondering over useless maps and discussing everything in terms of probability, and bar and restaurant staff who, if they are any more local than the tourists themselves, are sick and tired of being used as human versions of Google Maps. Even Dora had to acknowledge that answering the same questions hundreds of times per hour might get on their nerves eventually.

It was almost an hour later when a small calle opened up into a large square with a shining white church and bell tower. A stone well stood in the middle and there were far fewer people about than they'd encountered thus far. Dora recognised the place immediately.

"Campo Santa Maria Formosa! We're almost there."

And without further ado, she launched herself forward across the square. Taking the latest in a succession of long, thin calli, then another one, she finally stopped, jubilant, in front of… nothing!

Well, it wasn't exactly *nothing*; just a small space amongst tall buildings called Campiello del Tintor – the Little Square of the Painter. A leafless tree displayed a rather self-congratulatory sign announcing "The most beautiful bookshop in the world" and pointing towards a rather anonymous door.

Etta grimaced suspiciously. Dora and Leon marched in, and Etta, despite her doubts, had to follow. True friendship demands putting aside your fears – at least, sometimes.

ETTA GASPED.

She stood still, unable to make sense of what she was seeing. Turning right to left, left to right, and sticking close to her companions, she moved further inside what looked like a long tunnel.

There were books all over the place. Which is what she would expect in a bookshop, but there was something weird here. Maybe it was because most of the books were piled up horizontally, as if to make the best use of all the room available. Maybe it was because these piles were quite literally

2. A Christmas Mystery in Venice

everywhere. Maybe it was because of the sheer volume of books; as far as Etta could see, they reached from the floor to the ceiling. Well, almost. They were stacked on platforms raised fifty centimetres or so from the floor, probably to defend them from the sea that was likely to flood the place during the acqua alta, but they certainly went all the way up to the ceiling. Etta couldn't see the shelves, so many books were there.

But no, it wasn't just that which made the shop weird. There, in front of her, in the middle of the long corridor between the books was a real black gondola. And that was filled up with more books. Etta assumed that in the rising tide, the gondola would float and the volumes would be saved.

And – would you believe it? – in the next corridor were two ancient cast-iron bathtubs, enamelled in white, and they too were filled up to the brim with…. guess what? More books, of course. "English poems" a sign explained. As her hands browsed through, Etta recognised Byrons and Brontës, Rossettis and Keatses. In front of the two bathtubs were wooden basins in various sizes. Maybe they had once been used for wine making, or had the larger ones been bathtubs too? Whatever the case, they were resting on the floor or, if small, on old chairs, and they were filled up with hundreds of books. Mysteries, to be exact. In one, Spanish authors; in the next one, German authors; in the next…

Hanging on the wall among the multitude of books was a kayak. Postcards on the side showed what types of books this contained: some depicted Venice; others told of Corto Maltese, the sailor adventurer created by Hugo Pratt, who had been simply fascinated by the floating city.

A light at the end of the corridor attracted Etta's attention. A balcony was perched over a canal, and a joke sign said, "Fire Exit", showing a man in the water waving his hands. That was funny, especially as at that very moment, a gondola passed by so close, Etta felt as though she could have touched it if she had stretched out her hand. Which she did, but only to rest it on a green armchair placed between the fire exit and a couple of basins.

Sitting comfortably in the armchair, Etta noticed on the floor next to it a couple of books featuring Corto Maltese. She picked up *Fable of Venice*, set in 1921. Browsing the pages, with their fabulous drawings of Venice's most hidden places, she then raised her head to take in the view over the canal.

Etta was soon so absorbed in her reading, she almost didn't hear a little voice calling for her attention.

"Mrs? Hey, Mrs... that's my book and my chair!" the voice repeated. Finally, Etta looked around and found a child staring at her with determined blue eyes. Maybe nine or ten years old, she had a bunch of freckles over her nose and cheeks, and two long pigtails of light-brown hair on either side of her head. So peremptory was her request that for once in her life, Etta didn't feel like protesting.

"It's a nice place to sit and read," she said as she got up.

"I know," answered the child, her lips and eyebrows in serious straight lines. "I only went to pick another book – I left the Corto Maltese ones next to the chair so it was clear it was occupied."

"With all the books spread everywhere in here, I didn't realise these were there as a reserved sign."

The child had retaken her seat and Etta left her, wondering where her two companions might be. Not finding them, she walked from the back of the shop to the entrance and asked the cashier if she'd seen a woman and a Basset.

"I certainly saw them come in, but I haven't seen them leave."

"But I've come all the way through the shop from the back and I couldn't find them anywhere." Etta felt worried; if those two had run into trouble the very moment she left them to their own devices, it wouldn't be the first time.

2. A Christmas Mystery in Venice

"Have you checked the courtyard?"

"Nope. Where's that?"

The woman pointed to a little exit in the middle of the long corridor of books. Etta had not explored the area, thinking it led to a place reserved for staff. To the courtyard she went, and she gasped at what she saw.

Four red-brick walls were literally upholstered with large books. Looking like old encyclopaedias, they had been used to form a staircase that went up to the top of the tall walls, where even more books formed a balcony. Writing on the side of the staircase said, "Way Up", and more at the top promised a "Wonderful View". And people were actually climbing the book stairs.

Looking up to the balcony, Etta saw the back of a woman in a green cloak, beside her a Basset Hound, front paws resting against the top of the wall. Both figures were looking at the view, apparently lost in their own thoughts.

"Napoleon! Dorotea Rosa Pepe! What are you doing up there? And walking on top of books!" These last words were spoken as if it were a cardinal sin. "How could they place them outside in all this rain, damp and tides and..."

Leon barked, not out of pleasure at seeing his other biped, but because he resented being scolded. No way was a Basset ever deserving of such treatment. Then, he let sweet-biped-number-two explain to always-jumping-to-the-wrong-conclusions-biped-number-one.

"Mrs Passolina, how dare you think I would walk on top of books that are to be read? These are books meant for pulping, of course. The staff inside try to salvage books of all sorts, but these family encyclopaedias are out of date without being old enough to hold any interest as antiques. Yet the staff have even managed to give these a second chance. So instead of being an old grump, come up here and enjoy the view."

So, for the first time in her 60-plus years of life, Concetta

Natale Passolina stepped up a staircase made from dozens of books, and then stared out onto one of the strange and heart-melting watery views for which Venice has no equal in the world. And as if that wasn't enough, Dora asked a nearby tourist to take a picture of the three of them standing at the top of the book staircase. Leon expanded his chest for his many fans; Dora smiled her sweetest smile; Etta grimaced as the wind blew some of her red hair in front of her glasses at the wrong moment.

"So, did you find your *Pippi Longstocking* book?" asked Etta once they had finally left the book lovers' heaven.

"Of course I did," said Dora proudly, "a beautiful hardback edition from the 1970s. I also found *The Secret Venice of Corto Maltese* – it's an unusual guide, suggesting seven different itineraries within Venice – including one in our sestiere, Castello – with plenty of illustrations. Our walk is called 'Door to the Sea' – each itinerary is like a door to a hidden part of Venice. As soon as we're back home, I'll work this itinerary into our plans for tomorrow. There's also 'Door to Travel', an invitation to explore the most beautiful islands in the Lagoon. Some of them I had never heard of before…"

And as they walked and chatted, and chatted and walked, of course, they lost their way.

3

GONE!

When the two women and one dog found themselves by the sea, looking out over a strange island surrounded by red walls and sombre cypresses, Dora announced it was the St Michael graveyard. From there, she suggested, it'd make sense to take the vaporetto, rather than trying to make their way home on foot. Despite her horror of riding the open sea, undoubtedly much worse than the contained Grand Canal, Etta was too tired to protest. As for Leon, he loved the vaporetto. It was nice to have a long walk, and then enjoy a ride back home. What a treat!

Finally, the trio arrived back at the Biennale Gardens after their long unplanned detour. Now, they were hungry and tired, and Calle delle Ancore greeted them with delicious smells coming from many of the kitchens. It was well past lunchtime, but still the sweet perfume of food lingered in the air.

But it was not only mouth-watering scents that were coming from the windows. A sharp cry resonated, shattering the silence of the peaceful street.

"She never turned up? What do you mean?"

Etta didn't even have time to ask Dora if she too had

recognised that voice before a woman came rushing out of a red door, crashing into them.

"Giustina!" cried Dora. "What's happened?"

"Celeste! Celeste has not come home!"

"Is that your daughter? Was she at school?"

"There are no lessons on a Saturday, but she was supposed to go in for the Christmas play rehearsal."

"Maybe she's just late," said Etta, not sure what all the panic was about. Venice didn't seem a particularly dangerous place, even if you did get lost in its labyrinth.

"Or maybe she's at a friend's house," suggested Dora. "You know what children are like…"

"That's where I'm heading now," said Giustina, starting to walk away.

"We'll come with you," said Etta generously. But Leon stopped stock still, as if his four paws were glued to the ground. To make sure he got his point across, he planted his bottom on the cobbled pavement. That was an ominous sign: it meant the dog was using his hidden superpower. There'd be no way to drag him out of position as this hound could multiply his weight tenfold.

The two women were by now experts in dealing with Leon's stubbornness. They didn't even try to use brute force. Instead, Dora squatted down unsteadily and whispered into his ear.

"My gentle dog, I know it's way past lunchtime and you deserve your hard-earned meal, but it seems this woman – and more importantly, her child – really need your help."

So sweet was the biped, so urgent the call that Leon not only sprang to his feet, but trotted rather than walked behind Giustina. Not that you should expect much from a trotting Basset, but it was still fast enough for him to catch up with the woman.

Giustina had already turned the corner into Calle de le Furlane and was knocking on the window of a ground-floor flat.

2. A Christmas Mystery in Venice

A woman opened the door and she and a child joined Giustina outside. No, they explained, Celeste was not there, and no, she hadn't been at the rehearsal either.

Giustina, her voice quivering, said, "I spoke to her teacher, who also hasn't seen her today. In fact, she told me that Celeste hasn't turned up for any of the previous rehearsals either. For the past few Saturdays, she's left home saying she was going to school, but she never arrived, and she never intended to. Is that true?" Giustina addressed the last words to the neighbour's child, her eyes fixed on the young one. The child was worried, Dora and Etta could read it on her face, so her answer was truthful, not that of someone lying to cover for a friend.

"Celeste said she could not take part in the play this year as she was too busy helping you back home. She told us that you were expecting guests for Christmas and needed her help, so she never auditioned for any parts in the play or came to the rehearsals."

Giustina's expression was overwhelmed by panic.

"I'm sure nothing bad has happened to her," said Dora. "Maybe you can think of what else she might be doing, where she might be. Is there anything she likes, but may feel reluctant to tell you about?"

"I really can't think of anything. We need to go to the police – she's never disappeared before or gone to strange places without telling me first." And Giustina marched off along the calle. She clearly knew exactly where she was heading.

"Will the police be receptive?" asked Etta, her brain racing as she scampered, panting, after the woman. "After all, it's only a few hours since you last saw her. Shouldn't we go to her school first?"

"The police will have to listen to me. As for the school, if her teacher and friend say she wasn't there, there's no point going to look for her there now. We'll be wasting our time."

"Do you have any pictures of your daughter with you? Even if they're on your phone. The police will need them."

"You're right," said the woman. "I'm sure I've got plenty on my mobile." Giustina stopped to make sure she had actually brought her phone with her. With shaky hands, she then browsed through the pictures, showing them to Etta and Dora, as if for confirmation they were what the police would need. "I've got printed ones at home, too. Should I go back and fetch them?"

"These ones will do…" Etta was speaking as if she were an expert on police procedure, when suddenly she grabbed the phone from Giustina, her words following her actions like the boom of thunder trails behind a flash of lightning. "Gosh, give that to me. Let me look closer."

"What for?"

Etta closed her eyes and shook her head as if not believing what she was seeing. But there was no mistaking the straight brows over the serious blue eyes; the bunch of freckles; the long brown hair; the thin determined lips.

"I have seen this child. She was in the Acqua Alta bookshop just after one o'clock, busy reading in an armchair right by the canal."

"Celeste at a bookshop? Was she alone?"

"Indeed, she was. Is she a keen reader? Have you maybe forbidden her to read certain books?"

"She likes reading well enough, and no, I've never complained about her books. Anyway, maybe she's still in the bookshop."

"That's where we need to go," said Etta with a resigned sigh, "although it will take a while to get there."

"Not at all, follow me," cried Giustina, launching herself in a new direction. Then she paused and turned back to Etta. "Was she just reading?"

And Etta told the woman the little she knew as Giustina,

turning right and left, brought them to a canal filled with boats.

"Bepi," she addressed a man sitting with a few others on a group of chairs outside a bacaro, a typical Venetian bar, "I need your help. I'm looking for my daughter…"

Minutes later, the three women and one dog found themselves in a small but powerful motorboat, speeding along the canals, slaloming around the slow gondolas, and every now and then accelerating against the current and the winds. But mostly, the boat was jumping up and down in the waves as if riding a bull in a rodeo… at least, that's how it felt to Etta.

After what seemed like a long time of suffering, Etta and her companions left the boat in the canal and entered the front end of the bookshop. The woman at the till was the same one as Etta had spoken to earlier – her name tag told them she was called Sofia and she was the owner of the shop. When she asked if she could help, Giustina showed her a picture of Celeste on her mobile and asked if Sofia had ever noticed the child. The woman only had a brief look before confirming that she had.

"Yes, I saw her this morning. I noticed her because we don't get many children coming in alone."

"Is she still here?"

"I've not seen her leave, but it's a long time since she arrived." As she said this, Sofia left the cash till, calling an assistant to stand in for her, and led them along the corridor, heading to the fire exit and the canal. But once they got there, the armchair was empty. They spread out, looking in every nook and cranny of the shop, only to meet up again a few minutes later back at the entrance.

"She must have left when I wasn't watching," concluded Sofia. "But why do you ask?"

Giustina explained what had happened.

"I see," said Sofia. "What about you, Margherita?" she asked her assistant. "Have you seen this child?" And the woman called Margherita was shown Celeste's photo.

"Yes, Sofia, I saw her earlier, sitting near the fire exit. But when I went down that end to eat my sandwich at two o'clock, the chair was empty. In fact, I sat there to enjoy the view onto the canal. Maybe she went to the courtyard, or just made a quiet exit…"

"So strange I didn't see her," Sofia murmured, as if speaking her thoughts out loud. "I've been at the desk all the time, and there were enough customers to prevent me getting engrossed in a book… which would be the only likely reason I would have missed her leaving."

"What time did she arrive?" asked Etta.

"Late this morning. Around eleven thirty, I'd say."

"I saw her after one o'clock, so she stayed quite a long time," said Etta. "But by two o'clock, she had gone."

"Correct," said Margherita softly.

Etta, Dora and Giustina returned to the fire exit. Dora picked up a couple of books from near the armchair: *Fable of Venice* and *Secret Venice*.

"The same guidebook as I bought," she said with the smile typical of someone discovering a kindred spirit with the same taste in books. "I think I have also read the other one back home; I've always been fond of Corto Maltese."

But Etta was too busy exploring the fire exit area in search of telltale signs and clues to listen to her friend. Her inspection included going down on all fours and leaning out over the canal, as if she suspected the child might have fallen into the water.

"She's a good swimmer!" cried Celeste's mother, her voice horrified.

"And was she alone all the time she was here?" Etta asked. Sofia and Margherita looked at each other, nodding. They confirmed that they hadn't seen the little girl speaking to anyone. She had come in all alone, and in all probability had left alone.

"But she did speak to someone," said Etta. "Me. You didn't

2. A Christmas Mystery in Venice

see that, did you?" Before either shop owner or assistant could reply, Etta's attention was distracted by Dora murmuring something. What was the woman on about now?

"Hmm, I don't know," muttered Dora, her eyes glued to a page of one of the books she'd picked up. She'd been silent during Etta's examination of the fire exit and mini interrogation of the shop staff. "Had someone else done it beforehand… or was it Celeste? Or a combination of the two?"

"Was it Celeste what?" asked Giustina, looking over Dora's shoulder.

"See here, the last passage from *Fable of Venice* is highlighted."

Giustina looked disappointed. She obviously wasn't in the right frame of mind for books right now, but Dora continued nonetheless.

"It's a beautiful passage… and I heard someone else quoting it recently. Though at the time, I didn't realise it came from this very book."

"A passage from a book? Just what we need," said Etta sarcastically. She didn't mean to be rude, but she wanted to help Giustina and was concentrating on working out how the little girl could have vanished without anyone seeing her.

Despite her friend's apparent lack of interest, Dora read the passage: *"There are three magical and hidden places in Venice, one in Calle dell'Amor dei Amici; a second near Ponte de le Meravegie, a third in Calle dei Marrani at San Geremia in the Ghetto. When the Venetians are tired of the established authorities, they go to these three secret places and, opening the doors at the bottom of those courtyards, they go forever to beautiful places and other stories."*

"Are these places real?" All of a sudden, Etta was eager to know more. She had not expected Dora's discovery to reveal something this precise.

It was Sofia who answered without hesitation. "Well, at least two of them are. As for the third one, Calle dei Marrani, some say it's a hidden door in the Ghetto; according to others, it was inspired by Salizzada St Giustina in Castello."

"We'll have to check all four places, then, to make sure," Etta said. "Can you help us trace them on this map?" She waved a hand at Dora, who pulled a map of Venice from her bag and held it out to Sofia.

Giustina was dumbfounded and clearly struggling to follow the conversation. "Why would my daughter lie to me for weeks, and then disappear to visit some unfamiliar places all by herself?"

"This is the only clue we've found," replied Etta dryly.

"Most of us had a desire to escape our everyday lives when we were children," said Dora. "And actually, not only when we were children; we sometimes want to do the same as adults too, only now, we just can't. I think the allure of a magic door taking her to a better place…" Dora realised how brutal that may sound to the child's mother and changed tack somewhat. "Do you think Celeste suffered from some form of bullying?"

"Oh no, I don't think so. She's always been so calm and sociable."

Sofia handed Dora back the map with all four places highlighted.

"If your friend Bepi can take us in his boat," said Etta bravely, turning to Giustina, "it would make our trip much quicker."

"I'm sure he will," said Giustina. With that, three women and one dog ran to the front of the bookshop, crashed out through the door and sped towards the boat, map in hand. At the moment they reached it, Giustina's phone rang.

"It's Nico, one of Celeste's friends," she muttered, answering the call. Etta, Dora and Leon heard her surprised exclamation, then she half swallowed an exasperated scream, moderating it to a cried demand.

"Tear the letter open and read it to me!" She listened for a

2. A Christmas Mystery in Venice

few moments, then asked Nico if he knew exactly where Celeste was. Finally, she cut off the call with a nervous gesture.

"Celeste left a letter with Nico yesterday and told him to deliver it to me at lunchtime today. The boy forgot."

"What's in the letter?" Dora and Etta cried as one.

"Celeste wrote that she wouldn't be home for lunch today, but not to worry about her. She'll be back this afternoon and explain everything."

"No mention of where she was going?" quizzed Etta.

Giustina shook her head.

"Is there anything special about today?" asked Dora. "Some kind of anniversary, maybe?"

"No, not at all. Tomorrow is the second Sunday of Advent. But hang on... today..."

"Today what?" Etta asked, noticing a little uncertainty in Giustina's voice.

"Well, today happens to be her father's birthday, but we've never celebrated that. He wasn't there for Celeste's birthdays, so why would we mark his?"

"Where is the man?"

"In Vienna, as I explained..."

"Are you sure?" Etta insisted.

"Well, I've not spoken to him for almost a year. Why do you ask?"

"I believe someone passed the balcony at the back of Acqua Alta bookshop on a boat and picked Celeste up from the fire exit. That would explain why no one saw her leave."

"Oh my goodness, she was kidnapped! I knew I should have informed the police first..."

"Then we'd still be at the station, trying to explain that three hours ago, a child disappeared. No, first let's go and check those three, maybe four places the bookshop owner mentioned. There's got to be some connection. Was your husband fond of the works of Hugo Pratt?"

65

"Indeed, he had a large collection," replied Giustina, looking stunned.

"There you go," said Etta, reluctantly climbing on board the boat. "I don't know why, but I'm inclined to start with Calle Amor dei Amici. A place dedicated to the love of friends sounds the most likely."

They showed Bepi the map and where they were heading. The boat cut through the waters slowly at first as they were in a small canal, but once they reached the open sea, Etta felt she was likely to throw up, such was the frenzied bouncing of the vessel. Leon stood on the bow, enjoying the rush of the breezy air on his face. Dora sat next to Etta, her nose deep in one of the books from the bookshop. Then all of a sudden, she jumped up and sprang towards Bepi.

"Stop! Stop! Please, stop the boat."

The man did so, looking panicked as if fearing there was some kind of emergency like a woman (or dog) overboard. Etta felt grateful – had her friend realised how sick she was feeling? But there was a child to save from her rascal of a father. Celeste had mentioned in her note that she would return home this afternoon, but none of Giustina's neighbours had called her to confirm the child was safe. This was most likely a vengeful kidnapping, the villain telling the child they'd only be taking a nice, short boat ride together.

The roar of the boat's engine slowly died down. Finally, the others could hear what Dora was trying to explain.

"I think we should be going east, not west. It's not the three doors we're interested in – not the ones in *Fable of Venice*, anyway – but this one."

She opened *The Secret Venice of Corto Maltese*. The others looked at her without understanding.

"Each itinerary in this book is called a 'door to', whether it be to the east, travel, colour, whatever. One itinerary is called 'Porta del Mare – Door to the Sea', and it's in Castello, our very own sestiere. The day we arrived, when I went out with Leon, I saw a man stop in front of an arch in Biennale Gardens and pronounce the very words I read to you at the bookshop," and she repeated what she had heard. Then Dora stopped as the others looked at her doubtfully.

"He was at the beginning of this trail," she added, marking with her finger a point on the map near Biennale Gardens, "close to that arch, which looks like it opens on to nothing. But from there, you can jump into any Venice you wish – it's also the starting point of the Castello itinerary…"

"Seems a bit too farfetched to me," mumbled Etta, her forehead as furrowed as Leon's tended to be.

"You know where that itinerary ends?" Dora said self-confidently, knowing full well that Etta didn't.

Leon barked in approval. "Woof, woof, WORRRRF!" He knew the sweeter biped was on the right trail; her body language made it clear, even if she tried to hide her hound-like excitement. He could read her bearing: her nose was in the air, her back straight, her head up. And mostly, he could smell impatience ebbing out from every pore in her skin. If she'd had a tail, it would be furiously flogging her own flanks from right to left and back.

"What did the man look like?" Giustina asked doubtfully.

"Oh, it was too dark to make out details. I'm sure he was tall and thin, but that doesn't matter." She repeated feverishly, "You know where this 'Door to the Sea' itinerary ends?"

"No, we don't!" Etta replied for all the other beings, human and canine, on the boat. "Please enlighten us."

For an answer, Dora showed them the map in the book. Etta's eyes followed her friend's finger as it moved all the way from the gardens in the south along a long contorted route towards the north. Only after an infinite sequence of twists and turns did the finger stop at a vaporetto pier not too far from the sea.

"Celestia Pier," Etta read incredulously.

4

DOOR TO THE SEA

When they left the boat at Celestia Pier, Dora almost jumped out onto the pavement. Leon prudently waited for Bepi to help him out and Etta decided to be just as prudent, asking the man to lend her a hand too.

Even native Venetians find it impossible to know every calle, square or monument in Venice. Thus it was Dora rather than Giustina who led them. Her nose almost touching her map, she indicated the correct route and the others simply followed her. That was until Leon detected a scent too similar to Giustina's to be ignored. He howled with excitement, adrenaline coursing through his body, and his fast walk turned into a trot, the trot into the funny sort of gallop for which Bassets have an unprecedented reputation, looking almost like missiles ready to take off with the help of their flapping ears.

The group left the Fondamenta Case Nuove for the long Calle degli Orti, discovering their road barred by a tall and not so straight bell tower. They turned on to a series of narrow calli, some closed off by the canals. Then, after one more crooked bridge, they found themselves among a group of red-brick houses, and there Leon stopped abruptly, slamming on

2. A Christmas Mystery in Venice

his brakes and causing the bipeds to bump into each other's backs.

A red-brick arch, or rather, a secret door – one of the amazing doorways in Venice that open… well frankly, on to nothing at all – was ahead of them. Sitting on the low step below the arch, two figures huddled together, their backs turned, keenly chatting to one another. From the direction of their heads, they were looking forward… again, seemingly at nothing at all.

Moving silently closer to them, the three women and one dog started to hear their passionate voices, catch a few distinct words. And yes, even the pragmatic Etta could tell that beyond the doorway opening out on to one of many Venetian adventures, the two figures could see things other than those that normal eyes would catch. Busy dreaming of a bright future, they were talking of days to come, of things to do together.

"Celeste!" Giustina could hold herself in check no longer. Before anyone could blink, she was embracing her child as if to shield Celeste from malign influences.

"Hello, Giustina," the man said, his voice low and calm. Standing up, he revealed himself to be tall and thin, and he had the same blue eyes as Celeste. But his messy hair was dark – as much as was visible under his mariner's cap, anyway.

"You devil!" Giustina was seething. "What are you doing hanging around my daughter?"

"She's also my daughter," he wasn't challenging Giustina, just giving her a soft reminder. "A tiny bit, that is."

"Mum, we rode all along the Arsenal and discovered so many things. Then we started our walk, jumping through the door in Biennale Gardens and landing in another Venice…"

"Didn't you stop to think – you and your irresponsible father – that I might be worried when you didn't return home?"

"That's why Dad said we'd have to jump back, here at Celeste's door. I asked him to stay out a little longer, but he said that you'd get worried and that adventures are only good if one knows when it's the right time to stop. And I asked Nico to give you a letter so you wouldn't worry… He did give it to you, didn't he?"

"Yes, thirty minutes ago!"

"Oh, that stupid idiot!" cried Celeste, railing against her absent-minded friend. But Giustina was no longer listening to her daughter; she was looking spitefully at the man.

"You've been meeting her all this time, Giacomo, and never thought to tell me? The teachers at school informed me she's not been to any of the rehearsals, despite Celeste telling me that was where she was going. She lied to me, and to her friends…"

"I know, it's not right," said the man called Giacomo. "But whenever I tried to call, you simply refused to speak. I wrote and you never replied. So I decided I'd start with Celeste, try to speak to her…"

"I came up with the rehearsal idea, Mum, so we could meet on Saturday mornings without you getting worried. Only today, Dad had to work and could only see me later…"

"Why did you go out so early, though? Why did you spend so long in the bookshop?"

"It would have looked strange if I suddenly didn't go to a rehearsal a few days before the Christmas play. And I needed a reason to get out of the house anyway…"

"Lies!" Giustina rounded on Giacomo again. "That's what you've taught her, how to tell lies so she can do whatever she wants to…"

"That's not true!" Celeste protested. "Dad made me promise we'd tell you everything before the play. Of course, we'd have to as it would have given the game away when you came to watch me in it and…"

"You didn't give me much of a chance to speak to you," the man repeated softly, his eyes searching his former wife's. Giustina opened her mouth to protest, but something in Giacomo's intense gaze seemed to urge her to listen.

2. A Christmas Mystery in Venice

"I won't tell you I've turned into a saint, but five years have gone by and I've learned so much. I deserve your contempt, I'm not saying you're wrong. Just give me a chance to see my daughter every now and then, and help you if you wish."

"I don't need your help... especially once or twice a year when you can be bothered. That's not the same as being a full-time parent, whatever a stupid court order might say."

"Oh no, I don't intend to go to the custody courts; I've decided to move back to Venice, but you will set the rules on how often I can see Celeste. There have to be times you're busy or need to go to Mestre and can't leave her alone. I will be there for you now."

"Mum, please let me have a dad every now and then. He's funny and he can tell a good story, though he's not too good at timekeeping."

The last remark couldn't fail to make Giustina smile, as much as she didn't want to. Her eyes moved from Celeste to Giacomo, and from Giacomo to Etta – the woman who knew what useless cheats men were.

Giustina's surprise was clear to see when Etta nodded.

"Give him a chance," Etta said. "Either he's a talented actor, or he means what he's saying. But mostly, you owe it to your daughter. And finally..." here, Etta paused for a long time, as if she herself were a renowned actor in front of a gasping audience. Dora nodded, a large smile crossing her face from ear to ear. At times, Etta knew exactly what to say.

"Finally?" Giustina prompted.

"It's the time of year," Etta continued at last, "when we all need to remind ourselves of the healing power of forgiveness."

Leon had to have his say too. Had they forgotten he had skipped a meal in order to bring love and peace back into the bipeds' world?

"Woof, WOOF, WORF!"

3. DEVILISH DEEDS IN THE ALPS

THE HOMESWAPPERS MYSTERIES - A SHORT STORY

1

A WINTER TRAIN RIDE

Concetta Natale Passolina, or more simply Etta, felt at peace with the world. For once. She was sitting snugly on her comfy train seat, looking through the window at the wintry scenery outside.

A blanket of fluffy white snow covered everything, making the valleys, even the imposing mountains, look as peaceful as she felt. Every now and then, a castle would appear perched on the rocks, conjuring up long-forgotten tales she had heard as a child.

Oh, the joy of not having to drive for once!

Her friend Dorotea Rosa Pepe, generally known as Dora, looked just as enchanted. Her nose was glued to the train window, though every now and then she had to move back a tiny bit as her breath fogged the glass, hiding the view. As for Napoleon, the Basset Hound who tended to be referred to less grandiosely than he desired as Leon... well, he was busy sleeping. Snoring between the four legs of his two bipeds, he wouldn't bother with sentimentality of any sort. Not only was he not particularly fond of landscapes, unless they formed the backdrop to a real walk, but the train ride had proved to be a great disappointment. Not one single she-dog in his carriage, just a stupid pug who had the temerity to be a useless he-dog. And worse than that, he barked and panted at Leon whenever the larger dog came into his view. How rude!

As far as Etta was concerned, the uncharacteristic quietness of Leon increased her sense of wellbeing. It gave her the opportunity to look scathingly at the wee pug's human companion whenever he barked and annoyed the other passengers, showing how proud she was of her own dog who only barked for good reason. For now, at least.

Clickety-clack, clickety-clack, went the train. Etta's eyelids suddenly felt so heavy, she could no longer resist closing them. Her head dropped onto her sternum with neither resistance nor consciousness, banging from right to left and left to right in complete abandonment, mirroring every movement of the train.

A not-so-slight snore was escaping her lips when an abrupt voice broke into her pastoral dreams.

"It's not working!" a bear exclaimed. Or maybe it wasn't a bear, but a man with a long bushy beard, its thickness enhanced by the mane of hair surrounding his forehead. His hair wasn't particularly long, but it was wavy enough to make his face look rounder than it needed to. "The Wi-Fi signal has come and gone since we left Bolzano and I have urgent work to do."

"As you can see," the ticket inspector replied patiently, pointing to the snow scene outside, "we're not exactly in the middle of a city…"

"But if you say there is a Wi-Fi system on board this train, I expect it to function!"

"I apologise, but it is what it is. Is there anything else I can do for you?"

"You can find out if the Vipiteno library will be open today, and then I want to know about a museum in Colle Isarco, too. What are the opening times?"

3. Devilish Deeds in the Alps

"You mean the Ibsen museum?"

"That's the one."

"I'll do my best to find out," the inspector said, moving on to the next passenger.

What a demanding moron, thought Etta. *He's clearly an attraction collector, must make sure he doesn't miss a single one.* He'd woken her up for nothing, and now he was muttering on, railing against the train company. Even Etta's unintended pun couldn't bring a smile to her lips.

Really, certain people are just too much.

They were arriving in Vipiteno when the ticket inspector approached the obstreperous passenger as he was preparing to leave the train. Etta wondered fleetingly if the inspector had managed to obtain the information the bear-like man had asked for, but she soon dismissed the thought, preferring to look at the cute houses and a strange tall tower looming over them.

"That's the Tower of the Twelve," whispered Dora softly as the train pulled out of the station, carrying them on to Colle Isarco. "It's there to separate the old town from the new, which is not very new, as a matter of fact."

"They should call it the almost-new town."

"It was built at the end of the fifteenth century…"

"Then the no-longer-new-at-all town would be better."

"Whatever, Mrs Passolina. Either way, we're going to visit it as it hosts one of the best Christmas markets in the whole South Tyrol…"

"What are you doing?" asked Etta. As she was speaking, Dora had got up from her seat and was taking her scarf, hat and coat from the rack.

"Oh, you silly woman," Dora replied, laughing. "Our stop is coming up. Colle Isarco is only ten minutes after Vipiteno and we've still got to collect our cases from the luggage rack near the entrance to the carriage, which always makes me a little anxious."

"Colle Isarco?" Etta was so used to counting on Dora's organisational skills, she hardly bothered to ask anything before they travelled, apart from which country they were heading for.

"That's where we leave the train and take the bus to St Antonio."

Now Etta was shocked. The thought of stepping out of the warmth of the train to get on a draughty bus was less than appealing, and since they had left Bolzano, the landscape had been getting increasingly wild, the mountains taller and sharper, the snow cover thickening. Beyond Vipiteno, the changes in the surroundings had become even more alarming.

As Etta put on her coat and followed Leon, who in turn followed Dora, it dawned on her she was heading into the very heart of the South Tyrolean Alps in December of what was forecast to be a rather snowy winter. Luckily, Dora had insisted they take an early train from Trento, where they had left their car at her cousin's place. A wise decision: that had been the last place they'd seen the brown and green of the land before the snow covered it all.

Leon's demeanour showed that he was in total agreement with Etta, his ears drooping more than ever, his eyes sad. The platform at Colle Isarco was deathly cold, despite the pale morning sun doing its best to cast a modicum of warmth. Only Dora had not lost heart. After asking the other disembarking passengers for directions, she led her companions out of the small station to their bus stop.

It was a pity Dora's determination couldn't last for long. No sooner had they set foot outside than she dropped both her bag and Leon's leash. Clasping her hands together, her slate-grey eyes shining, her mouth open in an impeccable "O" that even the

3. Devilish Deeds in the Alps

painter Giotto, famous for drawing a perfect free-hand circle, would have been proud of, the pompom on her woollen hat dancing in the air, she managed to stutter a few words.

"Oooh, Etta, loo-look at tha-that!"

They were on a hill, facing the upper part of the small town of Colle Isarco. Above the layers of traditional buildings and snow-covered roofs, a tall bell tower rose, its red onion-shaped dome contrasting with the forest of fir trees cloaked in brilliant white in the background.

"That's the Parish of Mary Immaculate," Dora said when she was finally able to articulate properly. "We should really pay a visit, not to mention the Ibsen museum…"

"Ibsen? Wasn't he a Norwegian playwright?"

"Indeed, but so fond was he of this valley, he visited over and over again – I believe at least seven times – to enjoy the place. He loved to hike before writing his plays…"

"If I lived in Norway and took the trouble to travel to Italy, I'd rather stay in Sorrento…"

"That's as may be, but we will visit his museum. Soon!"

"How about when we have no luggage to drag around? Maybe after we're settled in our malga." Although not totally immune to the sense of enchantment Dora felt, Etta was so desperate for the comfort of their new home, she could almost see and feel the crackling fire in the mountain hut.

"You're right and… hey, stop!" Dora cried, waving at a departing bus. It had been waiting for the passengers from the train to get on board, but the driver was now leaving the square. Obligingly, he stopped, confirming that it was indeed the bus for St Antonio, reopened the large luggage compartment for them to stash their cases, and then helped the trio to clamber in.

"How long will it take?"

"No more than 15 minutes, it's not too far."

Etta breathed again: she could easily wait for 15 minutes

before stretching out her legs in front of a fire and being served... what? A hot drink? Maybe something sweet, too; cold weather makes one so hungry, doesn't it?

AFTER MORE TREES, MORE FOREST, MORE SNOW, ENDLESS MOUNTAINS, the driver announced they were arriving in St Antonio.

"But where is it?" asked Etta.

"Here!" replied the driver, pointing to a few houses scattered among the snow drifts, buried almost up to their roofs.

"And there's a church too!" said Dora as they exited and fetched their luggage, standing back on the pavement to allow the bus to depart.

"Where?" Etta looked across the street. Behind more white banks was a roadside shrine to Jesus Christ, its roof groaning under a thick layer of snow that looked to be taller than the structure itself. Beyond that, the top of another bell tower emerged. This one had a pointed cusp with a stack of glassless windows, each one hosting a bell. As soon as Etta set her eyes on them, the bells started to play a musical combination of notes.

"A good omen, at last," Etta said. But, not for the first time in her life, she was wrong. Very wrong.

A tractor pulling a small snowplough approached them.

"Are you the guests staying at Malga Allschatz?"

"Indeed," said Dora, smiling as she envisaged the romantic Alpine farmhouse known in this part of the country as a 'malga'. Some malgas only welcomed visitors for a meal, but their destination was one that also offered a cosy bed for the night.

"I guess so," snapped Etta, eyeing the tractor suspiciously.

"Worf!" said Leon, unsure what the proper response would be for the occasion.

"Dora and Etta, I guess. And this is Leon. I'm Andreas, by the way. Mum and Dad are waiting for you in the malga; you can

3. Devilish Deeds in the Alps

leave your luggage with me and I will take it up later on. Leon can walk with you if he wishes; I've just packed down the snow on the path, so it's pretty solid."

Two pairs of dismayed eyes moved from Andreas and fixed on Dora, who went red, then chuckled.

"I thought," she whispered with a guilty grin that made Etta even more worried, "it'd be nice to have a little adventure and walk to the malga. It's not that far and we won't have to carry the luggage…"

"It will only take you about an hour and you will enjoy your lunch so much more for the exercise! But I have to go now." Andreas had finished loading the bags onto his machine and was climbing into the driver's seat.

"But we will get lost!" cried Etta, her daydream of warmth and comfort dissolving.

"You won't. The path is a forest road and it's well signposted. But you might need these small crampons to avoid sliding down where there's ice," and he handed the two women a pair of horrible prickly thingummy-bobs each.

"Crampons?" cried Etta, brandishing her pair at her friend as if she were holding a weapon. Dora was already sitting on the snow, fiddling the strange contraptions onto her shoes. Once she was finished, she helped Etta to do the same. As for Leon, he decided he actually liked the fluffy white stuff. After a couple of running dives and roll-overs, he was ready to go, strange wild smells enticing him.

Andreas left, waving his hands and pointing them towards the beginning of the path.

"Now, I expect an explanation, Miss Pepe," said Etta as the tractor growled on its way.

"There's not too much to explain. We've come all the way to Val di Fleres to enjoy some time in the snow, and this includes some very easy walks."

"Easy, my tooth," Etta growled in a fair imitation of the

tractor, eyeing the path disappearing eerily into the forest. "Why didn't you tell me anything about these walks if they're so easy?"

"I did, but you weren't paying attention. Actually, you told me to be quiet, saying that you weren't sure you'd live to see the next morning, let alone a trip in six months' time."

Etta could remember saying that, or something very similar, but the holiday had seemed so far away back in the summer.

"Then," Dora continued relentlessly, "you never asked me any more about it."

And that was that. Dora might come across as a people pleaser, someone one could bend to one's will, but the truth was that between a sweet smile and an innocent expression, the woman was extremely good at manipulating people. Etta herself had a reputation for being stubborn, strong-willed and having everything her own way, but somehow she always ended up doing exactly what Dora had in mind.

She sighed deeply, looking to Leon for support. But being the wisest of the trio, the hound had already resigned himself to his fate and was happily climbing the mysterious path.

It started to snow, large fluffy flakes dancing in the air as there was barely any wind to blow them around. The path was large and well beaten, and even Etta had to acknowledge it climbed very gently. All around them were Christmas trees, their branches, already bent under the heavy snow, now turning completely white as the last of their dark green needles were covered.

The walk soon warmed Etta and she started to feel contented, so much so it came as a surprise when a wooden sign announced they were midway to Allschatz Malga. Dora opened the thermos of hot tea and Etta felt that drinking something warm in their present location was the experience of a lifetime, despite snowflakes plunging into the liquid to melt and disappear almost instantly.

3. Devilish Deeds in the Alps

A traveller's life is full of surprises. *How strange*, thought Etta, *to find such peace and happiness in something as inconsequential as drinking tea.* When Leon, lolloping along ahead, turned back to see if his slow bipeds were still with him, so impatient was he to see what would come next, Etta felt sure the Basset was smiling.

2

THE ALLSCHATZ MALGA

The second part of the path was definitely steeper than the first and the two women both appreciated the assistance of the light crampons that prevented them from sliding all the way back to square one. When their hearts were pounding, their legs aching and their stomachs grumbling with hunger, they finally distinguished a wisp of smoke rising in the air from the constant flurry of snowflakes. Then the entire wooden mountain hut materialised, sitting beneath fifty centimetres of snow on its roof.

White haired with spirited light blue eyes, their hostess Kerstin invited them inside and welcomed them in German. This was a language that Etta had mastered to perfection and even Dora felt confident enough speaking German to hold a conversation.

"I'm so happy you're here," Kerstin said, hugging and kissing the two women. "And you, Leon. I hope you enjoyed your walk?"

"WoRRRf!" Leon recognised the woman who'd been their guest during the summer in Castelmezzano. The fun home-swapping scheme that his bipeds had joined allowed them to

3. Devilish Deeds in the Alps

exchange hospitality of all kinds with like-minded people all over Europe.

"From the warmth of Southern Italy to the cold of a Tyrolean winter, what a dramatic change of environment," said a deep male voice.

"Klaus!" cried Dora, recognising Kerstin's husband as he joined them. "You're both wearing the traditional local clothes," she added, referring to the beige leather trousers and green gilet on the man, the white apron over a sleeveless dark-green dress, which was pulled in and laced at the waist, flattering the woman's shape. Both costumes were completed by white shirts.

"It's so lovely and warm in here." Etta had feared the malga would be cold, only suitable for people born and bred in the harsh Alpine climate.

"Of course, we want to keep the cold outside, and the Stube does its job well," the man pointed to a majolica-tiled wood-burning stove at the side of the living room. After Etta and Dora had removed their shoes and jackets and dried Leon's paws in the cloakroom by the entrance, they went straight towards the Stube, sitting on the cushioned bench beside it and resting their backs against the warm tiles.

"I would offer you a cup of coffee," said Kerstin, "but it's almost lunch time."

"We'll just sit here for five minutes, and then we'll freshen up in our room…"

At that moment, a Persian cat peered languidly out from beside one of the sofas in the room, only his head visible. His liquid green eyes lingered on Leon, weighing him up. The dog returned the stare. He didn't like cats at all – such incomprehensible creatures – but still, a well-bred Basset must do his duty and greet another furry pet.

Leon approached the cat cautiously. When the feline didn't react, Leon went straight in to smell his behind. Then, the crazy beast did exactly what Leon had feared: he arched his back, doubling his size as his fur stood on end, and hissed as if he were a poisonous snake. Leon stopped, nostrils still twitching. At least the cat hadn't tried to attack his nose with his claws.

Feeling he'd done his duty, Leon concluded that the beast was just as unfriendly as every other cat he'd met. From now on, this Basset would ignore him. That's that.

"That's our Max," said Kerstin as the two-faced beast purred and wound his body around Etta and Dora's legs. When he jumped on Dora's lap, Leon barked in protest. Rude and hostile to him, the cat was now sitting on his human – this was indeed provocation. Still, Leon did his raging at a safe distance. As the humans laughed at his reaction, he just turned his back on them and closed his eyes. He didn't want to see any more affection lavished upon the sneaky feline.

It's a dog's life!

"So, how was your journey?" asked Klaus.

"It was such a brilliant idea to leave the car in Trento," replied Etta. "I doubt we could have driven any further than Bolzano."

While her friends chatted, Dora remained sitting with her back pressed against the Stube, caressing Max and looking around the wooden room. The simple sofas with plenty of cushions; the photos on the walls a mixture of family members and guests, famous and not so famous, but all happy; a series of pictures showing the malga at different times over the four seasons. She was surprised how the area could turn from a total whiteout to bursts of deep green and brilliant flowers in bloom. But what enchanted her the most were the red-and-white checked curtains, framing the snowy landscape outside the windows.

"Tomorrow," Klaus explained, "the weather should improve and you'll get to see the majestic Tribulaun and the Parete Bianca from that window."

3. Devilish Deeds in the Alps

Dora had studied the area enough to know those were the highest mountains in the locality at well over 3,000 metres.

"Is it only us staying?" Etta asked.

"At lunch, there will be just us and Lisa Kornprobst. She's out for a walk with Gabriel, her seven-year-old son, at the moment. The poor woman lost her husband early this year and this is the first time she's been back to our malga since becoming a widow. But she wanted her son to have fond memories of this Christmas and Saint Nicholas, whose story is an important part of our seasonal traditions in this part of the world. More guests will arrive this afternoon before dinner, which will almost be like a family meal. Most of us know each other well as they've been coming here for years."

AFTER LUNCH, DORA WENT TO HELP KERSTIN PREPARE THE DINNER in the kitchen. The newly widowed Lisa Kornprobst joined them while Gabriel went to his bedroom to do his homework. Etta buried her nose in a book, enjoying the warmth of the Stube and determined not to set foot outside again that day. Except that determination wavered when Leon woke up from a long nap and stared at her intensely. She tried to ignore him, but the dog's mournful gaze struck chords she didn't even know she had hidden within her. Resistance was futile when the dog moved to sit right in front of her, his head tilted to the side.

She finally broke her silence. "What do you want?"

The dog didn't budge.

"Is it pee time?"

A little gleam in the dog's eyes told the slow-witted biped she had made a lucky guess.

"Why don't you go to the kitchen and call your favourite human?"

Such provocation was too much for a dog to bear, even one imbued with saintliness. Leon had to react.

"WoRRRRf!" he said, which even this slowest-witted of bipeds should know meant *the women in the kitchen are doing something useful while you're lazing around here like a couch potato.* A dog's vocabulary tends to be rather succinct compared to a human's.

"OK, OK, but just a short pee. I will open the door and you go out and come back. Quickly!"

So they went to the cloakroom at the entrance to the malga, where the humans had left their jackets and shoes, and Etta opened the door. A fierce wind swept in, carrying a mini storm of snowflakes, but the dog went out cheerfully. Etta stayed inside, watching from the window and wondering if she was doing the right thing. What if something happened to Leon? What if Dora asked her where he was?

Five minutes passed and Leon had not returned. In fact, he was nowhere in sight. Etta opened the door and tried to call him without shouting too loudly in case Dora heard and found out she'd let the dog out on his own. Then something large loomed out of the snow – something far too big to be a Basset Hound. And it walked on two feet, not four. Behind the figure was a troop of other bipeds.

"Hello!" said a cheerful voice. "If I haven't lost anyone, my wife and children should be right behind me."

"Here we are, Daddy," cried two laughing voices at his back.

Etta was shocked. "It looks as if your wife is here too," she said, peering into the snowstorm. "You could have checked everyone was with you before arriving at the door…"

"I was actually hoping to lose one or two of them along the way, all the more dinner for me."

"Daddy!"

The family came in, sitting on the side benches of the cloakroom to remove their shoes. The woman introduced herself as Barbara, then took off her coat and hat and went to look for Kerstin, saying she wanted to announce their arrival and pick up their room keys.

"You didn't happen to see a dog on your way in, did you?" Etta asked the man.

"Only a blue wolf who wanted to eat my child, but then he realised how skinny she is…"

The child in question ran to her dad and kissed him, despite his bad jokes.

"Dad, there was no wolf, let alone a blue one."

Muttering something about wondering why she'd ever allowed Dora to invite a dog to join them in the first place, thereby depriving humans of any moment of tranquillity, Etta started the whole laborious process of dressing for the cold. She slipped on her balaclava, buttoned up her jacket, pulled her boots onto her feet, which meant tying all the laces. No longer a flexible youngster by any stretch of the imagination, she found it rather uncomfortable to manoeuvre herself into position to complete this job. Finally, she pressed her hat onto her head.

She had just got up from the bench, when…

"Worf, worf, WORF!" Leon was at the door, demanding it be opened immediately to let His Majesty in. But if the man and his two children had expected the grumpy muttering woman to reproach the cute Basset who entered the room, they were very much mistaken.

"Oh, Leon, there you are! I was starting to get worried," and Etta, in a most uncharacteristic display of affection, bent down to clean the snow from his long body and kissed him on top of his head. She then declared to the family that the dog was a useless fellow, but it was too late. The man and his children winked at each other, as if communicating silently that this woman's harsh words and mannerisms were not to be trusted as in reality, she was as soft as the snow falling outside, and a sight warmer too.

"She's like Granny Caterina," announced the little girl, chuckling, "always pretending to be grumpy at something."

They all laughed except Etta, who was by now feeling particularly touchy. Barbara, returning with the keys, looked quizzically at her husband, who just grinned back at her. Then he introduced the rest of his family.

"I'm Aldo and those two pests are Mattia and Marzia. I'm ready to swap them for your dog any time."

"No, thank you," said Etta. "As naughty as dogs are, they're still better – actually, much better – than children who have yet to grow up and turn into dreadful teenagers."

Someone knocked at the door.

"Good grief, have you left more of your children outside?" cried Etta in alarm.

"No, I am lucky enough only to have to put up with two. And just the one wife!"

Etta opened the door again. A group of three people stood in front of her.

"It's you!" cried Barbara. "Come in, and you, get out of the way," she added, pushing her own family into the hall, "or there won't be room for everyone in the cloakroom. But don't walk around too much in those wet jackets. We'll only stay here long enough to say hello." Barbara turned to Etta and introduced the new arrivals, pointing to each in turn. "This is Heinrich, Nora and young Erika."

Etta watched as the three children greeted each other a little circumspectly. She assumed it must have been a while since Marzia and Mattia had last seen Erika, but before long, they'd be playing around together like old friends.

As Nora removed her coat and boots to go and get her family's keys, much like Barbara had done, Barbara eyed her with admiration.

"Oh, Nora, you're looking wonderful," she cried. "As slim and fit as ever."

Nora blushed, but her husband hugged her proudly.

"She's a beauty, isn't she?"

"And Erika looks exactly like her mum," added Aldo.

"But you're such an awesome happy family." Maybe Nora felt she had to say something kind in return. Certainly Barbara, with her stork-like figure, truffle-shaped nose and large face, could never be considered beautiful, but there was definitely something generous and kind about her.

"We're working on it," she said, chuckling.

"Almost every day," added Aldo. Sniffing the air, soon imitated by Leon, he added, "I guess it won't be long before dinner is served."

"Nope," said Etta. "My friend Dora has been shut in the kitchen with Lisa and Kerstin the whole afternoon. It must be nearly ready by now."

"Then," said Aldo, "let's go to our rooms and get changed. Over dinner, you, the lady from Southern Italy, can tell us all about yourself."

Nora returned with her keys. As the families pulled their boots back on, disappeared outside and made their way towards the building next door, Kerstin addressed Etta from the kitchen and asked her to lay the table for fifteen people.

Leon looked at her. "Time to make yourself useful too," his laconic expression seemed to say.

"You've not exactly been working that hard yourself," Etta answered.

The dog rolled his eyes and sighed. Hadn't he just been outside in the cold, scrupulously marking every single vertical landmark of his new territory so that all the creatures in the Val di Fleres would know that Napoleon the Basset Hound had become the one and only emperor of Allschatz Malga?

Humans!

3

LATE GUEST AT THE PARTY

A s the guests were sitting down for dinner, Etta realised she had set a place for one person too many. Following the instructions of Kerstin, she had laid the table for 15 people, but there were only 14 in total. Kerstin, Klaus and Andreas; Lisa and Gabriel; Barbara, Aldo and their two children; Nora, Heinrich and their one. Finally, Dora and Etta herself definitely made 14. Or was Kerstin expecting someone else?

Kerstin met her gaze as Etta looked at the empty place and wondered.

"Mr Kotter told me he'd be here by six o'clock," she said.

Just then, the cuckoo clock on the wall started to sing. The children turned to watch the automated figures of three Tyrolean couples dance a ballet on the balcony of a model mill, the horses on the ground below them running around their fenced paddock while a waterwheel was turning on the opposite side of the building. As if on cue, the living room door opened and a man made his way in. His forehead and upper cheeks were red from the cold, but the rest of his face was concealed behind a thick beard. He had clearly already left his jacket and shoes in the cloakroom at the entrance.

3. Devilish Deeds in the Alps

"Woo-wooo-wooo-woof!" Leon charged as if he were about to eat the man in a single mouthful, only to stop short one metre from him, seeing how he'd react and if he had managed to scare him. Disappointingly, the man took no notice of such a ferocious Basset. He greeted the guests in the room while Leon went closer to sniff his legs, his tail now a blur of frenzied wagging as if they'd been good friends forever.

"Please, stay seated," the man said to the guests around the table. "I'm so sorry, but it took me a little longer than I expected to climb all the way up to the malga."

"I wish you'd allowed Andreas to pick you up," said Kerstin.

"Oh no, I really enjoyed walking in the darkness of the forest, and I had my head torch to guide me. And now I'll be able to do justice to your meal," he said, taking the free seat next to Etta. Now that his face was returning to its normal shade; now that the white ice on his beard was melting, revealing its dark brown colour; now that he was close to her, Etta was startled.

It was the awful man from the train!

Kerstin introduced him as Mr Peter Kotter, and the man asked to be simply addressed as Peter.

"We all know each other here," Klaus explained to the new guest, as well as to Etta and Dora. "It's been our tradition to spend the feast of St Nicholas together for the past few years." He introduced the three families, then looking at Etta and Dora, he told the other guests how he and Kerstin had met the two women.

"In the early summer, we stayed at theirs in the pretty village of Castelmezzano in Southern Italy. Now they've come to stay with us so we can repay their hospitality."

Peter Kotter nodded a greeting to Etta and Dora, but didn't seem particularly curious about them. The chat that had been flowing freely up until now suddenly felt a little stilted, a little awkward. Or maybe it was just that the people around the table were too busy eating the delicious food Kerstin and her helpers had prepared to bother with chitchat.

Then Klaus, in a valiant attempt to break the silence, launched into tales of World War Two. Kerstin raised her eyebrows, as if to say, "Not again, please", but her husband continued as if he hadn't noticed. Aldo had war stories of his own to add, ones he said he had heard from his grandfather. Even Kotter looked quite keen on the conversation now.

"It's strange how tales of a long-ago war can stay with us through the generations," said Lisa.

"Thanks to my grandparents," Aldo replied.

"I never met my grandfather," said Peter Kotter. "He was deported by the Nazis to one of their concentration camps."

"Was he a Jew?"

"No, but he was a partisan, and in 1943, this part of Tyrol became a fortress of Nazi control…"

"So you're from Tyrol too?" asked Barbara.

"Exactly," said Kotter, not looking like he wanted to share more.

"How could the people here support the Nazis?" Etta could not help asking.

"It's not totally their fault," said Klaus. "You see, people in the Italian South Tyrol had not been treated too kindly by Mussolini and the Fascists. They were forbidden from using German as a language; they had to be 'Italianised'. Even the names of valleys, mountains and towns were changed. No wonder, when the Nazis took over from Mussolini here, people thought it was time to get their freedom back. But my grandfather, along with many other partisans, realised the two – Nazis and Fascists – were not that different, language aside. I learned this from my grandmother – sadly, my grandfather suffered a similar fate to yours, Mr Kotter."

Lisa was nodding at her son to listen. "My husband Franz," she said, "never tired of hearing stories about the war."

3. Devilish Deeds in the Alps

In fact, everyone around the table was now listening, fascinated. Aldo told how the Nazis had been hiding art treasures and masterpieces in South Tyrol, including in the mines of Val di Fleres. These stolen treasures had been given as presents or sold at favourable prices to the Nazis by Mussolini under the pretext of putting them somewhere safe.

"I remember," Aldo continued, "reading about 119 tons of gold bullion and coins, from the Central Bank of Italy in Rome, hidden by the Nazis not too far from here."

"It was hidden in Fortezza," Klaus confirmed, "just South of Vipiteno. Three different people were given the keys."

"Really?" asked Mattia.

"Yes," confirmed Klaus. "Some of it left Fortezza before the war ended…"

"…and was never found," concluded Aldo.

"Just a legend, I suppose." Heinrich smiled, a deep dimple appearing on the side of his chin as he caressed Nora's hand.

"Oh no, it's well documented," Klaus said. "Also, some of the money that was found has since vanished."

"It was recently stated that was not so," Aldo countered. "That money was returned via different means and banks tracked and justified the whole amount. I read this in a Central Bank report not long ago."

"What else could they say?" insisted Klaus. "They will never admit to such a big loss."

"Especially," said Kotter, "since it may have ended up in the Swiss bank accounts of the Nazis who fled to Argentina after the war."

"Still, I have my reasons for believing some of the treasure is still here, in Val di Fleres," said Klaus mysteriously.

"Come on, Dad," said Andreas, laughing. "Don't pull our legs."

"I'm telling you the truth," replied his father. "You remember when we went to clear your grandfather's house in October?"

"Of course. Did you find treasure in the basement?"

"Nope, but I found a note from your great-grandfather Nicholas that might shed a light on the whole thing."

"And you kept it to yourself?"

"Well, it wasn't in plain sight. I found it in a folder and I only just started going through the boxes of stuff in the past two weeks…"

"Is this why," asked Lisa, "you mentioned a treasure hunt in the most recent emails when you asked if we were coming?"

Klaus nodded solemnly.

"Do you have a treasure map?" asked Marzia.

"I do indeed! I keep it with me at all times," said Klaus, patting a pocket deep inside his gilet.

"Are we going treasure hunting tomorrow?" asked Gabriel, jumping to his feet.

"Tomorrow morning, I will be busy on the farm, so we will go to the Christmas market in Vipiteno in the afternoon – and enjoy the St Nicholas celebrations, of course – but on Sunday, we're going hunting for treasure."

"Oh no! What are we going to do tomorrow morning?" asked Mattia.

"Nothing much, really," Andreas answered. "Just have a few runs on the sledges, make a snowman, and then in the afternoon, a visit to Vipiteno to see the Krampus. That is, if you dare!"

The children were elated at the prospect of such a list of things to do.

Kerstin and Lisa had laid a magnificent apple strudel in the centre of the table. Then a few candles were lit and flickered merrily.

"We're getting close to the Feast of St Nicholas," Kerstin explained.

Dora was so enchanted, she asked to take a picture of them all, strudel included. As the camera flashed, Heinrich let go two powerful sneezes that woke up poor Leon. The hound had been cuddled up near the Stube, dreaming of saving the most beautiful she-Basset from a powerful avalanche. Even as he'd awoken, he still felt her warmth at his side, only to realise once he turned that it was the useless cat, Max.

Ouch! Life could be such a source of disillusionment, even for the bravest of hounds. But then Erika, clearly a kindred spirit, handed him a piece of speck she'd saved from her dinner plate. Slightly smoked, the cured ham tasted divine.

The pleasant surprises weren't over yet for Etta and Dora, either. Andreas got up and took up his accordion, while Klaus fetched his guitar and a fiddle for Lisa. Soon, rhythmic melodies filled the room, some sweet and nostalgic, some cheerful. Barbara and Kerstin sang along, inviting the children to do the same.

When Heinrich urged Nora to join in, it turned out the woman had an unexpectedly melodious voice. She wasn't loud, but her voice rose effortlessly above the others. Closing her eyes during her performance, she looked as if she was really feeling the music deep inside. Even Kotter, who'd been rather indifferent to the group's interactions so far, listened to her in clear admiration.

WHEN ETTA AND DORA WENT TO BED THAT NIGHT, THEY HAD plenty to discuss and share.

"What a surprise to find that awful man here…"

Dora looked at Etta in surprise. Maybe she had been in one of her raptures, maybe simply sleeping, but she had not noticed Kotter on the train.

"He asked about Colle Isarco and the very museum you want to visit. Let's make sure not to go there at the same time."

"Come on, Etta, maybe he's not that bad. Here, people tend to be much more reserved than we are in the south."

"Hmm, Kerstin and her family are friendly enough."

"And Lisa, she's such a sweet woman…"

"Well, I haven't managed to talk to her that much yet, neither at lunch nor at dinner."

"I have, in the kitchen. She seems vulnerable, as I guess she's still recovering from the sudden death of her husband, but at the same time, determined to find her way in this new life for herself and for Gabriel."

"I certainly can't read Nora, she definitely seems reserved …"

"That is, until she sings. She's got such a great voice, I had goosebumps listening to her."

"Her husband, on the other hand…

"…seems quite open and sociable."

"The bragging kind, I'd say. He shows off his wife and daughter as if they are supermodels."

"But they're both really pretty. As for Aldo and Barbara, they're simply wonderful, happy and cheerful."

"The most likely suspects!"

"Suspects?"

"In a murder mystery, I mean. The snowed-in hut, a certain number of guests, some historic evil lingering in the air. What a perfect setting!"

"Mrs Passolina," said Dora, chuckling, "what an awful mind you have."

4

WHAT BOOK WAS SHE READING?

Early the next morning, Dora was up, helping Kerstin to prepare the breakfast. Etta took Leon for his morning walk; she and Dora had agreed that it was best for her to stay a safe distance from the kitchen and any attempt at cooking.

Kerstin's face wasn't wearing its usual happy smile, so Dora asked if she was OK.

"Oh yes, it was just a stupid dream. I ate a bit too much last night, I guess, because of the celebrations, and I'm no longer used to digesting such rich dinners."

Dora laughed. "And you don't live in the part of Italy where we routinely have dinner at nine o'clock."

Kerstin smiled too, but as she broke eggs into the frying pan, some of the contents ended up on the hot hob. Within seconds, the acrid smell of burned food lingered in the kitchen.

"The other guests are coming over," said Dora, looking out from the window to the accommodation block.

"The children will be ravenous!" said Kerstin.

"Achoo, achoooo, ACHOOO!" A sequence of powerful sneezes announced that Heinrich was on his way. Dora raised her eyes and saw him and Erika just behind Barbara, Aldo and their children. By the time the trays of ham and cheese, tomatoes and cucumber, home-made muesli and yogurt, bacon and eggs were ready, most of the guests had arrived at the table.

"Mr Kotter, where is he?" wondered Kerstin out loud, doing a quick head count.

"And Nora," Heinrich said, turning to his daughter. "I thought we'd find her here, honey. Would you go and look for Mummy?"

Dora pressed her hands on Kerstin's shoulders, encouraging the woman to take a seat.

"I will help you search for your mummy, Erika, and we can look for Mr Kotter, too," she said. "Don't you worry, Kerstin, have a little rest. By the way, do you need me to fetch you something warm, Heinrich?" asked Dora, fearing the man might be getting a cold. His sneezes out in the snow had been so loud and his green trousers looked damp up to his knees.

"No, thank you," he said. "Hot coffee will suffice."

Dora and Erika went out of the malga into the cold and hurried over to the building next door. They checked the two bedrooms, but without success. Meeting in the corridor, they looked at each other.

"Mum is not in her room," Erika whispered, something strange in her expression. Was it just worry or could it be fear? Or was she, Dora, too prone to flights of fancy this morning?

"And there was no reply from Mr Kotter, but don't you worry, we will find them," she said, smiling at the little girl. The child smiled back.

"Come on, come with me," Dora said, leading Erika towards the barn close to the rest of the farm where she'd seen Klaus feeding the five small goats and a few chickens the family kept. They peered in. There was no one there right now, but they saw where Klaus had been cutting the wood for the Stube into small pieces to get the fire started. The axe hung next to a pile of kindling, and all around, the barn walls were hidden behind firewood, stacked side by side with a beautiful sense of order that made the tough job look as though it had been easy.

As they turned away, they saw Mr Kotter marching towards the entrance of the malga. He spotted them and waited for them.

"We were looking for you, breakfast is ready," said Dora.

"I was having a little walk beforehand to work up an appetite," said the man, looking at his boots and trousers, which were covered with snow. "The air around here is splendid and the view breathtaking."

Dora raised her eyes to the Tribulaun, the majestic mountain on the other side of the valley. Shaped like a smaller version of the Matterhorn, it was completely white and shining against the blue sky. Then she remembered the child beside her.

"Please, Mr Kotter, do go in. Erika and I will join you shortly, we're searching for Nora. Did you see her at all?"

The man shook his head and hurried inside. Dora held the door open for him before turning to the little girl.

"Shall we check the visitors' room, near reception?" The reception building, which Kerstin had told Dora was mostly used in the busy summer months, was an area of the property that she and Etta hadn't yet had the time to visit. Kerstin had also mentioned a visitors' room: a sort of library, with plenty of books about the area, where guests could enjoy reading in silence rather than the chatter of the living room.

And it was here that they finally found Nora, busy browsing through the books.

"Oh, Mum," said Erika, running towards her mother. "We were looking for you, Dad was wondering where you were."

"Breakfast is ready," Dora added.

"It's OK, honey. Let's go," said Nora, almost mechanically putting her arm around the shoulders of the girl. All the while, she kept her eyes lowered, as if she was too preoccupied with her thoughts to pay attention to her own daughter. Or was the perfunctory hug a way to lead Erika away from the library shelf

Nora had been browsing? Dora made a mental note of the woman's position when they'd entered, resolving to check it out next time she was in the library, only to laugh at herself an instant later.

Etta's ways are getting under your skin, Miss Pepe, she chastised herself. *It's none of your business.*

"Come on," she said to mother and daughter, "let's go and get some breakfast."

"We were waiting for you!" cried Gabriel as soon as the trio entered the dining room.

"My apologies," said Nora. "I was having a look around. No matter how many times we visit the malga, I still find the whole place enchanting – our bedroom, the barn and the views. I simply lost track of time and didn't realise breakfast was ready."

Heinrich shrugged indulgently. Looking at his wife, he said, "You need some food before you start your wanderings. Sit and eat, then we will spend all the time you wish outside."

THE DAY PASSED QUICKLY. DESPITE KERSTIN ENCOURAGING HER TO go outside and enjoy the clear day with the others, Dora insisted on helping her to prepare the lunch. Dora was pleased to see that the other woman seemed much better now: Kerstin moved around the kitchen faster and with more determination than she had earlier. Within an hour and a half, everything was ready.

"You'll be able to cook a variety of Tyrolean dishes when you go back home," said Kerstin, laughing.

"I can't wait to invite the Castelmezzano folks round to enjoy such a treat," replied Dora as she finished taking notes in her recipe copybook.

The children came in, rosy cheeked and buzzing with excitement after their morning of sledging with Andreas. But not long after lunch, they grew impatient and started to ask questions about when they would be going to Vipiteno to see the Krampus. The adults told them to wait, to have a little afternoon nap first, but they soon gave up all attempts to get the children to calm down.

"Mattia, you insist on going to see the Krampus," Barbara teased him, "but if I remember rightly, they terrified you last year."

"Oh Mum, last year I was just a child. Now it's different."

Marzia laughed at her brother. Erika seemed uncertain what to do – did she want to go? She looked at Gabriel and the boy nodded his head.

"Mattia's right, we need to face up to the Krampus!"

Etta and Dora were a little surprised at such perplexities. Lisa must have caught their questioning looks as she explained.

"You see, the Krampus are a weird experience. They're not like meeting Santa Claus and the good elves."

"Not at all like that," Gabriel backed his mother up. "Krampus are quite scary."

"You never know if they're going to use their whips," Mattia whispered.

"Frankly, I'm never sure whether to take Gabriel to see them," said Lisa, looking at the children.

"But they need to learn about the good *and* the bad," said Nora.

"Come on," urged Barbara, chuckling. "it'll be fun."

DORA FOUND VIPITENO SIMPLY ENCHANTING. THE GRANITE TOWER of the Twelve was decorated with small lights all the way up to the top of its 46 metres. Both the Old and the New Town, situated on either side of the tower, were made up of a succession of pastel-coloured buildings, their *erkers* – the typical oriel bay windows – an ingenious way for the people of olden times to capture light and save money. In the Middle Ages, the taxman charged the residents depending on how much of their window faced the square. For this reason, the buildings tended to be tall and thin, making the most of their narrow outlook.

Below the *erkers* were beautiful porticos housing mostly independent shops. Not one arch was without its garland. On the pastel facades of the buildings, some windows had been painted with large numbers as if the whole town was a giant advent calendar. And, in fact, each window did have something surprising to reveal: a wreath; an unusual garland; an angel; a red and green ribbon.

As for the town square itself, it hosted a number of stalls, their roofs covered with a thick layer of snow. Vendors were selling handcrafted Christmas items, from cute wooden animals to a collection of angels that delighted Dora and left her uncertain whether she could ever choose one over the others. Woollen scarves and gloves, wooden toys, blown glass decorations for the Christmas tree – everything was tantalising.

Most importantly, many stalls were offering cooked food that tasted home-made. Dora and Etta tried the traditional fruit bread and warm apple juice spiced with a touch of cinnamon, while Leon was handed a piece of sausage by the cutest blonde woman. Even better, a black and white she-cocker caught his eye. Although not as pretty as the she-Basset of his dreams, she was certainly an enchanting animal.

Dora understood the dog's desire for romance. She stood and chatted with the cocker's biped for some time, while Leon did his very best to conquer the heart of the beautiful creature. Unfortunately for him, though, it was almost six o'clock and the children were shouting that it was time for St Nicholas to make his appearance from one of the *erkers*.

Leon protested. This was an emergency, he'd have to use his superpowers. He sat down, multiplying his weight tenfold, a handy trick that in the past had taught Dora and, more

3. Devilish Deeds in the Alps

importantly, the ever-impatient Etta not to even try to pull or, worse, drag him. They wouldn't budge him an inch.

Dora was terrified they would miss all the fun. Sweetheart though he could be, Leon could also become the most stubborn creature in the world when he set his mind to it. But Etta, to Dora's surprise, had a sinister smile painted on her face.

"It won't work this time," she said.

In response, Leon looked at her defiantly, certain in the knowledge that he would win this particular battle. Etta asked Dora if she could take his leash, then she invited Leon to move. The dog pretended indifference, looking elsewhere – towards the she-cocker, mostly. Then Etta did something that would usually have proved as stupid as it was pointless: she started to drag the hound. Only this time, the outcome wasn't at all what Leon had expected.

5

ST NICHOLAS AND THE KRAMPUS

The packed down and frozen snow was the perfect surface for sledging. Before he knew what was happening, Leon felt his bottom sliding over the ground, apparently with no great effort from the human. Getting to all fours, he stood stock-still, but his paws slid merrily across the square, the people assembled there smiling and laughing at the spectacle. Eventually, he and his bipeds arrived under the window where the children were waiting.

Etta smiled at him, Dora chuckled, and Leon reckoned he had never felt so humiliated in his short but wretched life! As for the she-cocker, she had totally disappeared from sight. And he had almost won her heart. Humans, contrary to popular canine folklore, are not a dog's best friend.

The children, unmoved by the sorrows of the young hound, were full of expectation. Finally, the clock chimed six, the window opened and Saint Nicholas himself appeared. He greeted the children, asked if they had behaved well during the past year, what exactly they had done wrong if the answer was no, and made them promise they'd do their best to be wise for the year to come.

3. Devilish Deeds in the Alps

"Now, it's time for me to announce who's been the most generous and brave child this year. I can see him right there, I never forget a face," and St Nicholas indicated the area where the Allschatz Malga guests were gathered. "But I can't remember his name. I've written it somewhere," and he clumsily unrolled and browsed down a long scroll of paper held in his hands. "There we go... Gabriel. Gabriel Kornprobst has been through a challenging year, knowing sadness no child should ever have to experience. But he has been brave and generous, supported his mother, helped his friends at school, and never forgotten to share his weekly pocket money and, more importantly, a kind word with a homeless person he often sees not far from his school. Well done, my child. May you be an example for all the children in this square, in this country and on the planet."

Gabriel went red, looking like he couldn't believe his ears. He was invited to join the saint up on the balcony, where he was appointed as child of the year. The watching folks clapped their hands and shouted his name; Mattia, Marzia and Erika were evidently proud to be his friends. For her part, Lisa could not hold back her tears, but they were joyful tears. Joy was something the poor woman wouldn't have felt much this year.

"How did he know?" she asked incredulously.

Kerstin winked at her, then looked at Klaus, who played dumb.

Dora caressed Lisa's arm. "You've been a splendid mother to him."

"I haven't done much, embittered as I have been by my own pain..."

"I'm sure you have not been embittered or Gabriel would have turned out to be a very different child. Your husband, wherever he is, must feel extremely proud of you both right now."

Lisa was just wiping away her tears when a horrified cry resonated from beside the Tower of the Twelve.

"The Krampus! The Krampus are coming!"

The children became scared and excited at the same time. The crowd moved to either side of the square and, along the pathway that opened up, a series of dark silhouettes came forward, their gait irregular. When they were close enough for the lights to pick out their features, Dora felt chilled to the bone. Etta was quite impressed, although she'd only admit that to herself, and Leon decided he'd stay behind his two humans since they offered something of a barrier between him and the scary beasts. After all, he lacked any better options.

Tall, hairy figures with formidable horns came forward, dressed in goatskins and wearing terrifying masks with phosphorescent eyes and protruding red tongues. The overall effect was so gruesome, they made the orcs from *Lord of the Rings* look like contestants in a beauty contest. But more scary than their appearance was their behaviour. They scanned the crowds; still picturing the world of hobbits and orcs, Dora was reminded of the nine riders searching for the Ring Bearer. Every now and then, a youth would rush from the crowd into the street and provoke them, at which the devils reacted wildly, trying to beat the bold human with their whips and block their return to the safety of their friends on the pavement. If no victim was available, then they'd continue their search of the crowds to a soundtrack of screams from children and adults alike.

All of a sudden, the crowd went deadly silent. Even the devils stood still. Then, from the end of the street, wild screaming broke out. A chariot illuminated by fiendish red lights and smoke appeared. This, Dora knew, was the coming of the Master Krampus. Larger and scarier than all the others she'd seen so far, he was shouting and growling as he drew ever closer, forging dangerous weapons with hammer and anvil in the flames of his fire.

"Oh my goodness!" she cried.

"The Krampus are the servants of St Nicholas," Barbara

explained. "This, the master of them all, is still a servant to the saint…"

"I wish St Nicholas had chosen nicer helpers."

"There can be no light without darkness," said Nora.

The hideous parade had nearly passed them when a figure hurtled from the crowds on the pavement. It was as if the unfortunate had been thrown onto the road in front of the devils. The Krampus reacted wildly, surrounding the man and whipping him as he tried to escape.

"Hey, that's Heinrich!" Kerstin shouted.

"Oh my goodness!" Dora cried again.

Nora and Erika stood frozen to the spot. The other children smiled shyly, uncertainly. Wasn't it all a game? Heinrich tried to escape them, but the Krampus had closed their circle around him and were pushing him from one to the other as if he were a ball. When he stumbled, their long arms, tapering into whips at the ends, reached for him…

The health and safety officials intervened at this point; the game had turned too rough. They freed the unfortunate victim – not without some effort – and the devils, laughing, moved on in search of their next victim before Saint Nicholas could call them off.

"Don't you worry," said Barbara. "It *is* just a game. It turns a bit wild at times, but Heinrich is fine… see? Aldo is with him."

And Aldo waved from the other side of the road, giving a thumbs up to show that everything was OK. Kerstin seemed to relax at that, the tension leaving her bearing. She smiled at Nora and Erika.

"I'd say it's time to get something to eat," she said. For tonight, the party from Malga Allschatz had reserved a table at one of Kerstin and Klaus's favourite restaurants in Vipiteno.

Dora, too, sighed with relief. It had all been very interesting, but she was glad when the Krampus disappeared from sight.

THE BUS DROPPED THE PARTY IN ST ANTONIO. FROM THERE, USING the torches Klaus had left under the bus shelter, they started their walk back to the malga.

"This night walk is part of the St Nicholas tradition, too," Barbara said, guiding the two Southern Italian guests along the slopes covered in snowy firs. "I'm sure our children will carry this memory for the rest of their lives."

"I prefer the memory of the presents St Nicholas is going to leave us during the night," Mattia said.

"This is why it is important to tire you out so you sleep soundly till morning," replied his mother.

"The Krampus won't come too, will they?" murmured Erika.

"Of course not," Barbara answered. "It will be just the saint, don't you worry."

Erika looked through the dark forest. Shivering, she stayed in between the grown-ups.

Dora let the women and children pass by and joined the men behind. Heinrich was explaining how some people from the crowd had pushed him into the street in front of the Krampus.

"What scoundrels!" said Aldo. "I guess they were working in league with the Krampus."

"Yes," confirmed Klaus, "at times, the games tend to get wild. When I was young, they were even wilder, but then it was youngsters vs youngsters. And the victim was always someone the Krampus knew well. At times, someone would want to take revenge on a particularly spiteful adult, but it was always someone from within the community. We would never usually even consider victimising a visitor. I'm so sorry for what happened tonight."

"What doesn't kill you makes you stronger," Heinrich replied dryly.

"Indeed," agreed Aldo.

3. Devilish Deeds in the Alps

Then there was a scream from the women.

"What now?" Klaus cried.

The men rushed forward. Dora, unable to keep pace with them, was left behind. From a distance, she could hear angry words being exchanged, but she was still too far behind to make out what they were. Thinking she heard twigs snapping in the dark forest alongside her, disappearing downhill in the direction of the town, she glanced around in anxiety. Her heart in her throat, she struggled to catch up with the others.

The whole group was circling around a tree. At its base was the mask of a Krampus. A small lantern to the side made the phosphorescent eyes shine and the tongue and ugly brow stand out.

"Andreas, was it you who left that thing here?" Kerstin cried. "Such a stupid joke!"

"It wasn't me, Mum."

"But that's my mask," said Klaus, bending down beside the tree and picking it up. The children moved back, scared and delighted in equal measures by the sight.

"Klaus?" Kerstin questioned him.

"No, dear, I didn't even think about playing a prank. I haven't seen that mask for quite some time..."

"Let's go," said Lisa. "Let's get back home."

"But this time," said Klaus, "let me and Andreas lead the way."

"Maybe it was Mr Kotter," said Dora.

"That would be even more stupid, being as he's had nothing to do with us all day long," replied Barbara.

When they arrived in their bedroom, Dora could see Etta was relieved to be back. Mr Kotter had returned to the malga a good 30 minutes after the group from Vipiteno. When asked whether he had left the mask out to give them a nasty shock, the man had denied even being aware of its existence.

"I've been in Bolzano all day long, then I had dinner in Colle Isarco. Now I'm tired and want a hot shower, not to play the fool," he'd snapped before disappearing towards the accommodation block and his room.

"The night walk in the forest felt good," Etta said now, "but for once, I agree with Kotter. All I want is a hot shower, or even better, a bath. Then a hot drink, then some warm snuggling under my blankets."

As Etta ran her bath, Dora quietly left the room and slipped out into the night. Maybe she was being foolish, but she was curious.

Reaching the building next door, she entered the visitors' room and switched on the lights. No one else was there. There were quite a number of shelves, each one full of books, but Dora was only interested in the one she'd seen Nora browsing that morning.

To her surprise, she discovered that the shelf contained the work of Henrik Ibsen. There were also biographies of the man, some literary critiques, essays documenting his stays in Val di Fleres. But one volume was sticking out by almost a centimetre, as if whoever had been reading it last hadn't had time to push it back fully to align with the others.

It was a play: *A Doll's House*. Dora remembered the story of the powerful drama. She browsed through the pages, jogging her memory.

"Oh, Nora, that's true. How interesting," she murmured. As she came to one of the last pages, it looked more rigid than the others, as if liquid had been spilled on it, leaving it hardened and the printed characters blurred.

Just above Ibsen's work was a section containing guides to the walks of the area and the history of the place, from the mines of the fifteenth century to World War Two. Finally, on the table,

3. Devilish Deeds in the Alps

she noticed a book that had been left open. She closed it so she could see its title: *History of Val di Fleres and the Silver Mines.*

Maybe the children have been doing a little research before the treasure hunt planned for tomorrow. But this wasn't the right time for that kind of reading. After all, she'd found out what she had come looking for.

6
IS SOMETHING WRONG WITH THIS MORNING?

When Etta woke up the next morning, it was late. The tiredness of the long day out had made her sleep in.

Immediately, she felt a sense of discomfort. Then she realised what it was. It was bitterly cold, while the previous morning she'd found her and Dora's room pleasantly warm.

She woke Dora, who jumped out of her bed. "Goodness, isn't it late? I should be helping Kerstin with the breakfast."

"Then you shower first. I will use the bathroom after you as Leon seems to be enjoying his bed this morning."

The dog raised an eyebrow and slowly wagged his tail, just so they'd know he was alive. Of course, he'd be ready to sprint, but not a second before the scent of frying bacon hit his nostrils.

When Dora entered the kitchen, Kerstin was busy. She was almost done with the cooking, but none of the guests had materialised in the dining room yet.

"Good morning, Kerstin, did you sleep well?"

"I did and feel much better for it."

"I will finish laying the table. Shall we call the guests?"

"It's Sunday, let's allow them to come when they're ready. I can keep the food warm…"

3. Devilish Deeds in the Alps

"Speaking of warmth, is there a reason why the malga is cold this morning?"

"Cold?" Kerstin asked, following Dora into the dining room. "I was sweating so much in the kitchen, I didn't realise. Could it be that Klaus has been so busy chopping wood, he forgot to turn the heating on? He got up at the same time as me." As she spoke, Kerstin opened the Stube, which was empty and cold. "Oh, that silly husband of mine. How could he forget?"

The two women put on their jackets and went outside, where they met some of the guests on their way to the dining room.

"I'm afraid Klaus forgot to switch on the heating, but luckily breakfast is hot and ready when you are."

"Don't you worry," Aldo said, smiling, "the treasure hunt will keep us warm."

"And I doubt these children even feel the cold," said Lisa. Mattia and Gabriel were rolling in the snow, Marzia was laughing at them, but Erika, as ever serious faced and doe eyed, looked around herself as if she felt lost. Etta and Leon were also out in the snow. But of Klaus, there was no sign.

Once Kerstin and Dora had told Etta why there was no heating, she offered the services of herself and the hound in the search for Klaus.

"Did you check the barn?" asked Etta after they'd looked around the immediate vicinity without success.

"I shouted through the door, but there was no answer," Kerstin replied.

"I think we'd better go in and look properly," Etta said dryly. Only Dora spotted the note of alarm in her friend's voice.

Andreas, eyes still heavy with sleep, joined them and Kerstin told him what they were doing, and why. He too had noticed his room was unusually cold.

"Dad?" the young man called as they entered the barn. The only answer was a loud "Baa, Baaah" from the goats. Logs and splinters of newly chopped wood lay on the floor, proof Klaus had been there. Why had he left, leaving his tools scattered on the ground?

"Baa, Baaah." Despite their feeders being full, the animals seemed nervous that morning.

"What are these dark spots on the hay?" Etta asked. Slowly kneeling down, she touched them, only to recoil and withdraw her hand swiftly. "Do you keep the goats for their meat?"

"Of course not, these little goats are only for milk and cheese." Andreas reached out a hand and touched the dark spots. Bringing his hand to his nostrils, he exclaimed, "Blood!" He stood up, horrified, and went behind one of the orderly piles of wood. The piles stood a metre or so forward from the wall, creating a small passage where the hay was stacked.

"Dad!" Andreas shouted. Etta and Dora followed him and found him bent over a body. Leon howled deeply, raising the alarm, while Andreas felt for a pulse in the man's neck.

"He's alive," he announced. Turning his father's head very gently to one side, he showed the others a cut on the back of his head. "Pulse and breathing are fine and there's not much bleeding now. I guess he fell..."

"Or he was hit on the head," said Etta.

"Hit on the head? You mean deliberately hit?" stuttered Andreas as if those words made no sense whatsoever.

"Yes. In fact, whoever attacked him most likely hit him, then dragged him behind here so we'd discover him later rather than sooner. Dora, stay with Andreas. I'll tell Kerstin to call the hospital and the police. Leon, come with me."

"Who? Who would hit Dad, and why?" cried Andreas, checking his father's pulse and breathing again, trying to bring Klaus back to consciousness without moving him around too much.

Once the emergency services were on their way, Kerstin ran to kneel beside her husband. Etta left the barn to gather all the guests in the dining room. There were three people missing: Mr

3. Devilish Deeds in the Alps

Kotter, Heinrich and Nora. Poor Erika had no explanation for the absence of her parents.

"I woke up when I heard the other children laughing outside. Neither Mum nor Dad was in the room."

"Lisa and Barbara, could you keep an eye on the children?" asked Etta. Barbara replied that as a trained First Aider, she would be better occupied having a look at Klaus. She would fetch a warm blanket to cover him up for a start.

Lisa nodded in approval. "Don't you worry, I'll keep an eye on the children."

"I'd better leave Leon with you," said Etta generously. "If you need anything, just open the door and he will run to fetch us."

Leon, happy to be allowed to stay as close to Heav… to the kitchen as possible, sat with an inflated chest. *Bassets are the perfect rescue dogs*, he thought. As the children surrounded him playfully, he added, *And babysitters, too*, a little less enthusiastically.

While Barbara, blanket in hand, ran to the barn, Etta and Aldo went to the accommodation building and knocked on the bedroom doors of the three missing people. No one answered. When Andreas and Dora joined them out of doors, Andreas had good news: Klaus had regained consciousness, so the young man had left his father in the care of Kerstin and Barbara. The latter had spoken to the paramedics on the phone, who had recommended they didn't move the patient, just kept him warm until the Alpine rescue team arrived.

"He's answering questions, and his answers make sense," Andreas added with relief, only to fall silent all of a sudden, abruptly stopping in his tracks as his eyes fell on the snow at his feet.

"What are you looking at?" Dora asked.

"There are two sets of footprints leaving the malga," the young man pointed out. He and his three companions walked along the tracks, careful not to obliterate them with their own footprints, until they reached the forest path leading out of the property's land. "You see? The first set of prints is going upward, and whoever it was, they took a sledge with them. The second smaller set goes downwards..."

"The larger prints could belong to Mr Kotter or Heinrich," said Etta. "The smaller ones could be Nora's. But where did the third person go?"

"I hope," said Aldo gloomily, "he's not been left dead, or wounded like Klaus."

"We need to get into those two bedrooms," replied Andreas, alarmed. "I'm going..."

"No, you aren't," said Etta bluntly. "Instead, follow this first set of footprints, staying out of the person and the sledge's tracks," she pointed to the prints climbing uphill.

Andreas did as he was asked, but his face showed he was puzzled by the instruction.

"You see?" said Etta triumphantly.

Now, two sets of tracks lay side by side. The footprints were roughly the same size, but the ones left by Andreas were clearly not as deep as the others.

"A second person followed the first, careful to walk in their footprints!" cried Aldo.

"Correct!" Etta confirmed. "So, Nora took the path down, and it's likely the two men went up."

"You're right," said Aldo. "And if you look at the sledge's track, it's not always regular. There were two people and two sledges."

"Well spotted," said Etta, pleased the man had caught on. "Now, Andreas, where is the old mine your dad mentioned on Friday?"

"I don't even know which one in particular he meant, but there are some tunnels on the way to the Mountain of Time."

"It's a difficult walk to the summit!" cried Aldo.

"But the mine entrances are way before the summit."

"We'll go as far as we can so that we can point the police in the right direction when they arrive." Etta was curious as a cat, but also prudent.

As Andreas went to fetch the gear they'd need for Alpine climbing, Dora voiced a concern.

"I don't understand why Nora took the other path," she murmured. Etta shrugged. It wasn't important now.

Upon his return, Andreas looked at the other wooden sledges at the side of the building, leaning against the wall.

"We'd better take two of the larger ones," he said.

Etta looked at him, horrified. She did not fancy sledging back down the mountain in the slightest, but after all, she could always walk down a path she had managed to climb up.

However, climbing up proved to be more difficult than she had anticipated. Etta and Dora soon realised they would be more of a hindrance than a help to the two men. After twenty minutes, they simply had to accept they should make their way back. But before they could suggest that very thing, their words were cut short by a weird swooshing sound on the path just above their heads. A matter of seconds later, something came sliding down the mountain at full speed. They had just enough time to jump off the track before Peter Kotter zoomed past on a sledge, a second one appearing close behind him. This one also passed them with no sign of slowing down.

"Is Heinrich trying to catch Mr Kotter?" asked Aldo.

"Kotter must have wanted the treasure all to himself, and he hit my father on the head because he had the map of the mines," Andreas must have been going over the who and the why during the entire climb.

"Heinrich," Etta added, "must have got suspicious and followed him."

"OK, OK, but shouldn't we go after them?" said Dora, who'd

been unusually quiet. "I doubt Mr Kotter has a mind to stop at the malga."

A reluctant Etta sat rigidly behind Andreas with Dora behind Aldo as the two sledges rushed down the path. The abundant snow packed down by the passage of the previous sledges and the freezing temperatures made the conditions perfect for them to slide as fast as the wind. Etta looked in horror as the many fir trees surrounding them whizzed by.

I'm going to be killed by a Christmas tree, she thought, holding even more tightly on to Andreas, *a perfect themed death for the season*. The wind hurt her cheeks and face, filling her eyes with tears, but the real reason she wanted to cry was sheer terror at the bends that Andreas took at breakneck speed, the sledge tilting as it climbed the banks of snow to the sides of the curves.

A launch pad to hurl us into the ravine, Etta thought, horrified. Where there were no bends, the sledge picked up speed again. It ran so fast that even the scariest roller coaster, something she usually abhorred, now seemed safe and gentle by comparison.

The path plunged down past the malga and the two sledges went with it.

When Etta's stomach was just about ready to admit defeat and fly out of her mouth once and for all, the steep slope smoothed out, the rush slowed down. After a couple more minutes, the forest path opened up and the valley floor came into view, with it the sight of two abandoned sledges. And further down, almost next to the main road, two men were fighting in the snow. From the valley foot, a repetitive "nee-naw" could be heard: reinforcements were arriving.

Etta realised Kotter was getting the better of poor Heinrich. Andreas and Aldo left the sledges where the track ended and ran over the snow banks to help him. Then suddenly, Heinrich landed a punch on Kotter's face. As the hairy man let him go, the tables were turned. Heinrich rolled on top of Kotter, pounding him with heavy blows. Apparently unaware that help

3. Devilish Deeds in the Alps

was at hand, Heinrich grabbed a large piece of hardened ice that the snowplough had packed into the roadside. He was ready to stab at Kotter with the lethal shard of ice when a large snowball hit him in the face, taking him by surprise.

As Heinrich let the rock-solid ice fall into the snow, Etta was all at sixes and sevens. It had been Dora who'd thrown the freezing missile at the man.

7

IS SOMETHING WRONG WITH DORA?

Etta stared incredulously at her normally gentle friend, who continued pounding Heinrich with a flurry of snowballs. At the same time, Dora was shouting at Andreas and Aldo, who had finally reached the two fighters. What she was saying sounded totally nonsensical to Etta.

"Stop Heinrich! He hit Klaus, and now he's trying to kill poor Mr Kotter."

Roaring with anger, Heinrich sprang to his feet, looking ready to fight all comers. But the distant cry of the siren was now far closer. Four police officers piled out of their vehicle as it came to a halt and, before Heinrich could blink, they had grabbed hold of him. Having snatched up the mean-looking shard of ice again, he did look the most threatening of the men. At the same time, the officer in command questioned everyone present on what was going on.

"That man," Dora explained, the uncharacteristic vehemence in her voice probably a result of the adrenaline rush from the mad chase down the mountainside, "has attempted to kill two people. One is recovering in the Allschatz Malga; the other one is this man here," and she pointed to Kotter.

"Actually, I thought the culprit was Kotter," Aldo stuttered. Despite having acted on Dora's instructions, he clearly had no idea what was really happening.

"It *was* him," cried Andreas. Etta watched a wave of fury cross his face. She was sure he was about to attack Kotter, who had struggled to his feet and, despite the bruises covering his forehead, was coolly dusting the snow from his clothes.

"No, you've got it wrong. You should arrest him," Etta shouted to the police officers, jabbing a finger at Kotter too, but her eyes were glued on Dora. She feared her friend might have completely flipped.

"Why don't you check that man's neck before you point the finger of blame?" Peter Kotter replied insolently, nodding his head in Heinrich's direction. "Just behind his hair."

Like a wild animal who'd been captured, Heinrich bucked and struggled, trying to shake off the police officers surrounding him. Three of them held him firmly while the fourth did as Kotter had instructed.

"A swastika tattoo," said Andreas in disgust, recognising the dreaded Nazi symbol.

"He's a member of the Neo-Nazi movement," said Mr Kotter, Dora smiling and nodding at him to carry on. "And he was keen to get his hands on the treasure rumoured to be in the mines." Mr Kotter kneeled down next to his sledge and extracted something half buried in the snow. It was a wooden box, partly ruined by the weather, the years that had passed, the humidity.

Heinrich was protesting, loudly. "He was the one who went to steal the treasure. I just followed him to stop him – don't trust what he says…"

"You hit Klaus on the head, Heinrich," said Dora with a seriousness and determination Etta hardly recognised. "I saw you going into the barn early this morning. You see, I was out too, walking the dog. That's when you must have hit Klaus and stolen his map. But I didn't realise what you were up to at the time, or I would have called for help straight away."

Etta's mouth dropped open as she stared at Dora in amazement. She could have sworn that when she awoke this morning, neither her friend nor dog had moved from their beds.

"You dratted nosey parker," snarled Heinrich. "I was sure no one saw me leaving the barn after I'd hit that stupid Klaus…"

The man stopped speaking abruptly, but it was too late. He'd already incriminated himself.

"What's in the box?" said one of the police officers. Mr Kotter looked uncertain whether to hand it over, so Dora again intervened.

"There's a wounded man in the malga. I'm not too sure how weak he is, but I believe it'd be a great comfort to him if we could unwrap the treasure in front of him."

The police officer who seemed to be in command informed Heinrich of his rights before ordering two of the others to take him away. Then he said he and the third officer would follow the little group to the malga.

"Wait one moment," said Dora, pointing to a figure who was walking in their direction. A bus had stopped, but the figure had declined to get on.

"Is that Nora?" asked Etta, befuddled.

"It is." Then turning to the police, Dora explained, "She's the wife of the man you've arrested, but she had no part in his crimes. In fact, I feel sure she will testify against him, or at least help with a psychological profile of the man."

"What's going on?" called Nora as she came closer. "Has something bad happened?"

"I will fill you in as we walk back to the malga," said Dora gently. "I'm glad you decided not to leave Erika."

"I couldn't," said Nora, her eyes fixed on the tips of her feet.

"Your husband has been arrested. He stands accused of attempted murder, and the police are likely to have some

3. Devilish Deeds in the Alps

questions to ask about his affiliation with a Neo-Nazi movement."

"Neo Nazis?" Nora looked shocked.

"Indeed. Have you never noticed that awful tattoo on his neck?"

"Of course, but he told me that was a stupid mistake from when he was young…" then Nora stopped, but her face spoke volumes. This harsh truth clearly explained many other weird things the poor woman must have noticed over the years.

"Let's go," said the lead officer and they started to walk towards the hut. As curious as she was, Etta felt this time, she'd better wait for explanations. She joined the men, leaving Dora to walk beside Nora.

"I'M SURE," SAID DORA SMOOTHLY, "YOUR LIFE WILL BE EASIER FROM now on, with that cruel man out of it…"

"Cruel, you say, but he's never been violent towards me," replied Nora as if weighing up every single word.

"But cruelty in a marriage doesn't necessarily involve beatings or any other kind of physical attack. It could just as easily be about controlling someone's personality, forbidding them to express themselves freely, threatening them or making them believe they're unable to cope with the world, to take responsibility for their own lives. Those forms of cruelty are equally brutal."

Nora looked at Dora, shocked. "How did you know?" Dora just nodded, but stayed silent, waiting for the younger woman to continue. "I don't know how it happened. It seemed when we first met that he was in love with me, but as soon as we were married, he started criticising everything I did. He'd use a condescending tone to put me down whenever I took the initiative, even when it came to bringing up my own child.

Slowly, I came to feel as if I were totally inadequate; that without him, I couldn't do anything. In this way, he managed to alienate me from my family – he never openly asked me to cut off my ties with them, but every time we met up with them, afterwards, he'd criticise everything they'd said and done, the influence they had on me and Erika.

"He was so strong and I so weak. When Erika was born, he insisted I quit my job. And that was the very end of my independence. When *I* was unable to give *him* another child – a male child – his behaviour towards me became even worse. He told me I was totally useless as a woman and a human being. Only when there were other people around would he pretend we were the perfect family. I can see that clearly enough now, but would you believe that all the time we were together, I thought everything was my fault?"

"I guess as a Neo Nazi, with all the narrow-mindedness that involves, he saw a woman's role as that of staying at home, doing her chores and producing heirs. He manipulated you bit by bit to fall into his trap of control – after all, the Nazis always have wanted to be in control and dominate other people, so they're often unable to develop healthy relationships. The love of power drives them to insanity. You were putty in Heinrich's hands, until... until you read Ibsen, I guess."

"How did you know?" asked Nora in surprise once again.

"When I saw you in the library at the malga, I confess I was a little nosey. I went back to check what books you'd been so absorbed in reading, you didn't even pay any attention to your worried daughter. Then I found a page in one of the books that was rather rigid and blurred, as if some liquid – maybe tears – had poured onto it, and I realised you didn't look at Erika that morning because you wanted to hide that you'd been crying. And what was that page but the final speech of *A Doll's House*? Where Nora Helmer finally opens up to her husband and claims her right to live her own life."

"A doll. Yes, I have been treated like a doll for years – something to own and show off to people – rather than a human being, let alone a companion. When I read that scene, I thought, like the other Nora, I would have to run away. I left early, very early, this morning, but then I thought of Erika…"

"And unlike Nora Helmer, you simply couldn't leave your daughter with that ogre."

"Do you think he was that bad?"

"He almost murdered a man this morning! Besides, he's killed your personality. You're still too close to what he's done to you, but with time, you will be able to see the whole picture."

"More importantly than anything, I hope I'll be able to take care of Erika."

"Of course you will, but do not hesitate to ask for help."

"I'm not sure my family…"

"They *will* be there for you. Also, I believe Lisa will be more than happy to support you."

"But she's got her own troubles. She's bringing up Gabriel alone now…"

Dora smiled. "That's why I see you becoming good friends. You can share all the difficulties, and the victories, of being single parents. You've got so much in common and she's a generous woman, someone you can trust. And don't forget Kerstin and Barbara, not to mention me and Etta. We don't live close by, but you're welcome to stay at ours anytime."

A sob rose up from Nora's chest. She hugged the older woman as if she were her dearest friend, and only once the sobs subsided a little was she able to stutter a few words.

"For the first time, I can see the hope of a real life ahead of me. Bless you."

The Alpine land cruiser that had carried the medical staff was parked outside the malga when Dora's group arrived. They found everyone, apart from Lisa, Leon and the children, gathered around Klaus in his and Kerstin's bedroom. To Kerstin's obvious relief, the medics had said that the wound to Klaus's head was superficial; it had just bled a lot as head wounds always do, helped by a nick to the upper part of the ear. Luckily, Heinrich hadn't used the axe, but an unchopped branch of wood. And just as luckily, the warmth of the hay that Heinrich had dumped Klaus in saved him from hypothermia while he lay unconscious. To be on the safe side, the medics would take Klaus to the hospital for further checks and keep him in for a couple of days, but on the whole, the man seemed to be fine.

On hearing this, Klaus refused to go anywhere until he had heard the whole story. At this point, all eyes fell on Dora, who turned crimson. But after clearing her throat a couple of times, she spoke.

"When Mr Kotter admitted to being the descendant of a family of St Antonio partisans, I guessed that a dislike of the Nazis would be inherent in him. But I didn't realise how deep it went until today. Ahem... perhaps, Mr Kotter, you would like to tell this part?"

The man looked as reluctant as Dora to take centre stage. All the same, he stepped up, telling how he had been tracking the moves of a Neo-Nazi organisation. This organisation was constantly trying to finance itself and had been eager to find the Nazi treasure rumoured to be hidden in Fortezza and the surrounding mountains.

"So is this why Heinrich visited us over and over again?" asked Kerstin.

"Yes." Dora nodded. "And when Klaus sent the email saying that he had discovered something that indicated there was indeed treasure hidden in the mines, Heinrich could not believe his luck. Since he arrived, he's been determined to get to the

3. Devilish Deeds in the Alps

treasure before the others, so when Klaus told the children he carried the treasure map with him day and night, he almost signed his own death warrant.

"I believe Heinrich also went treasure hunting yesterday morning. When I saw him coming out of the accommodation building for breakfast, his trousers were already wet."

"You're right," Nora confirmed. "I heard him go out when it was still dark on Saturday morning and he was very angry when he came back. I pretended to be asleep so he wouldn't realise I knew he'd spent a long time outside. I've learned not to ask him questions, not to notice things. Only once I was sure he was asleep did I get up and go to the library to read a particular book…"

Dora pressed her hands on Nora's shoulders to calm her.

"In the end, Heinrich had to act fast," said Dora, aware how curious the people around her – including the police officers and the medical staff – were. "He knew Klaus would have the map with him this morning, so he had one last chance to get his hands on the treasure before everyone started hunting for it later on today. So he followed Klaus into the barn and struck him over the head while he was busy cutting the wood. Klaus wouldn't have seen or heard Heinrich creeping up behind him, so he was easy prey."

"But how did he think he'd get away with it?" Lisa asked.

"Maybe he hoped everyone would assume there had been no treasure after all or that someone else had stolen it. I don't think many of his friends," and Dora looked at the folks around her, "suspected him."

"I suspected Mr Kotter," said Aldo, and the others nodded in unison. Then Aldo turned to Kotter. "Actually, how come you decided to follow him?"

"I…" Mr Kotter looked at Dora, as if asking for permission to carry on. "I like having my little walks early in the morning, so I saw him leaving the barn. When I realised he was taking a sledge and going up the mountain, I decided to follow him. I suspected he may have attacked Klaus," Kotter looked apologetically at the man in question, "but I had no time to lose. I knew Heinrich was up to something.

"Once I got to the mines, following his tracks as exactly as I could to cover my own, I noticed something odd about a stone in the side of the grotto's entrance. While he was searching in the depths, I pulled the stone out and… realised I'd found the treasure before he did."

Klaus almost jumped out of his bed. "So you have the treasure?" he asked.

Mr Kotter revealed the box and handed it to him.

"May I remind you," said the lead police officer, "that any treasure you find is the property of the Italian state…"

Klaus waved him away. "I never wanted to own it… that was not the point." His hands wriggled impatiently around the box. Kerstin came to his rescue, gently taking and opening the box. Inside was a torn cloth and Klaus unrolled it.

"Why wrap money in a rag?" Aldo wondered out loud.

But when Klaus had finished unwrapping the treasure, he revealed neither gold bullion nor coins, but a baby.

8
IT'S CHRISTMAS!

It was a beautifully crafted statue of a baby, cast in pure silver.

"The Holy Child!" cried Barbara.

"In the eighteenth century, the miners in Val di Fleres gifted this statue of the Holy Child to the church in St Antonio," Klaus explained. "But during World War Two, the local priest, helped by the partisans, hid it in the mines before the Nazis could get their hands on it."

"A number of treasures were stolen from Italy to enrich Hitler and Göring's personal art collections," said Barbara. "Some were hidden in the Alps, awaiting safer times before they could be delivered into the hands of their new owners. But why would they bother with the treasure of a little church?"

"Not Hitler and Göring, but a powerful Nazi was in command of the whole Southern Tyrol area. He too appropriated for himself whatever he could lay his hands upon…"

"But Klaus," asked Barbara, "did you know all along the map didn't lead to the Nazi treasure? The gold bullion Heinrich was searching for?"

The man smiled and nodded. "Of course. My grandfather

said in his note it was 'our treasure' the partisans had hidden, so it had to be something that belonged to Val di Fleres, not just an anonymous stash of gold."

"But we – Heinrich included – assumed otherwise…"

"When Aldo mentioned the Fortezza gold, I thought it'd be fun to let you believe that was what we were searching for, until we found the real treasure."

"Actually," Kerstin said, looking at Nora kindly, "it turned out to be a dangerous but lucky misunderstanding. Klaus got hurt, but he'll be fine, and Heinrich's greed and vile allegiances finally came to light."

"Now we have to confiscate the Holy Child," said the police officer apologetically. "But it will be handed over to the church in St Antonio as soon as possible."

"And it's time to take this man to the hospital before he gets even more excited," added the doctor from the Alpine rescue team, looking at Klaus.

"Let me just show the statue to Lisa and the children," said Barbara. "They will need to know all that has happened as I believe it will be an important lesson for them not to give in to greed or bigotry." She must have felt Nora's worried eyes on her, as she added, "Don't you worry, dear, I'll be very careful how I phrase everything. I promise it won't hurt Erika – she needs to know who her mother really is…"

"Her *mother*?" asked Nora, looking even more worried.

"Yes. She's been waiting all her life for you to reveal your true colours," and Barbara gave Nora a heartfelt hug before disappearing in the direction of the dining room.

KERSTIN AND ANDREAS FOLLOWED KLAUS AND THE MEDICAL TEAM to the hospital in Bolzano. Dora and the other guests reassured Kerstin that they would take care of the malga and the meals.

3. Devilish Deeds in the Alps

"Hey, but what about the Krampus?" asked Aldo after their hosts had left, clearly still trying to piece it all together. "Don't tell me Heinrich made it up about being shoved in front of them."

"Um, not exactly," said Mr Kotter. "I realised from a few telltale signs he was a Neo Nazi and I wanted him to reveal himself…"

"Which telltale signs?" said Barbara. "I never suspected."

"It was the dimple and the sneeze, wasn't it?" asked Dora.

"How clever of you!" Kotter chuckled. "And I thought you were a harmless little old lady."

Etta looked at them without understanding, as did everyone else.

"You see," said Mr Kotter, "we need to go back to World War Two again. In Bolzano, a couple of young Nazis were renowned for their cruelty to prisoners; one was Ukrainian, the other Austrian. The man who arrested my grandfather, tortured him, and then sent him to the concentration camps was the Austrian. In the local tales, he was described as having an unusual dimple on the side of his chin that made him look as if he was smiling all the time, even when watching people being tortured in front of him…"

"There must be loads of men with a dimple," Barbara interrupted again, "although I agree Heinrich's one was unusual."

"There's more. The Austrian was referred to as 'the sneezer'. Apparently, the man would descend into a flurry of sneezes every time he came from the darkness into bright light. Heinrich has the same affliction – remember how he sneezed when the flash went off on Dora's camera?"

"A sneeze?" said Aldo. "Come on, how can you identify a man from a sneeze?"

"Someone in my village suffers from the same thing," said Dora. "It's called ACHOO – don't ask me what the acronym stands for, it's a succession of long, difficult words. It's a strange and very rare affliction."

"And it is genetically transmitted. So the combination of rarity and genetics made me believe I had found the descendant of the man who treated my grandfather so cruelly."

"So you just happened to come here by chance?" Etta asked incredulously.

"Correct," said Mr Kotter after an almost imperceptible hesitation.

"What a story!" Lisa concluded.

But when they were alone outside, Dora and Mr Kotter had a very different conversation.

"I just want you to know, I don't believe for one moment you came to Val di Fleres by chance…"

"So, why does my quick-witted lady think I am really here?" Mr Kotter's beard moved slightly at the sides, telling Dora that the bear-like man was smiling.

"You were searching for the treasure… not the Nazi treasure, but the miners' Holy Child."

"You are destined to surprise me continually. By pure chance, a month ago in Neustift im Stubaital, just across the Val di Fleres, I happened to speak to a priest. When he discovered I had been born here, he shared with me the recollections of a churchman from St Antonio. He told me about this churchman helping two partisans to hide a precious silver statue of the Holy Child that the miners from the eighteenth century had forged. It had been invaluable to the community, but only the priest and the two partisans knew where it was. The partisans had been killed by the Nazis. The churchman had mentioned to the priest I spoke with that the treasure had been hidden in the mines, but death took him before he could reveal exactly where.

"You came over in search of more information, which is why Etta heard you asking for the opening times of the library in Vipiteno and the museum in Colle Isarco," stated Dora.

3. Devilish Deeds in the Alps

"After hours of useless research, I came to the malga – the only accommodation I could find in St Antonio at this time of year. And here I found Klaus, who boldly admitted he would be hunting for Nazi treasure. I knew as soon as Klaus mentioned his grandfather had been a partisan that it had to be the Holy Child he was seeking, not the gold bullion, and I couldn't believe my luck!

"And as well as the treasure, it seemed I'd found the grandson of the man who tortured my grandfather and sent him to suffer and die in the German concentration camps. Not that I wished to seek revenge against a man for the actions of his ancestor, but his own actions indicated that he wasn't so different. The way he spoke to his wife and his daughter was far too patronising. I started to observe him closely, saw his unpleasant behaviour towards his family when he thought no one was watching. Then, as he removed his jacket, I was sure I spotted a little swastika tattoo on his neck. Then I knew who I was dealing with. I simply decided to give him a hard time and threw him among the Krampus just for the fun of it."

"And the mask at the malga?"

"Well, that was a little childish of me, but I really wanted to scare him. I had only found that mask by accident. It was on Saturday morning; I had been looking for information in the hut library when I heard Nora coming in and I did not want to speak to her, so I hid in the store room. I came face to face with that awful mask before I could make my way out. It scared the life out of me!

"After he'd been the victim of the Krampus during the parade, I felt sure Heinrich would not only be just as frightened as I had been, but he'd also imagine the mask had been left there just for him. So I fetched it from the store room and set it all up, and then pretended I'd only got back to the village 30 minutes after you. You know the rest."

"The trouble is, I don't believe that you came to find the treasure to give it back to the community."

Kotter's beard moved as he smiled again. "What did I want it for, then?" he asked.

"Maybe to sell it. In fact, from the footprints we found this morning, I believe you, with the larger crampons, were the first to hit the trail. The indentations made by the crampons didn't go as deep as the rest of the footprints, which sank lower when Heinrich's footfalls packed the snow down further. After hitting Klaus, Heinrich followed your prints and knew he'd find you at the mine."

The man shrugged. "When he arrived, I had already found the treasure and walked backwards to my sledge in my own footprints. I was hiding in the trees. By the time he rumbled my little trick, I was heading down on my sledge."

"Hmm," said Dora, deep in thought for a moment or two. "Just one thing is puzzling me. How did you know where to look for the treasure? Did you discover something while we were all in Vipiteno yesterday? You didn't just come back to the malga for the mask, did you?"

"No," the man admitted. "During the Krampus incident, I realised Klaus wasn't wearing his Tyrolean costume and I had an epiphany: what if he had left the map in the pocket? Because of a certain… ahem, shall we call it professional bias?" Dora raised her eyebrows slightly; the only skill Kotter had shown so far was a tendency to help himself to other people's belongings, but she'd never heard a thief refer to himself as a professional before. Then again, she didn't make a habit of mixing with thieves as a rule. She kept silent as the man carried on. "I had kept a close eye on everyone's movements and I knew where Klaus put the malga keys. Not that they feel the need for much security up here. Entering his bedroom, I found the map exactly where I'd expected it to be and took a picture of it. Easy-peasy! The most difficult part was having to wait until morning as it was too dark

3. Devilish Deeds in the Alps

to go treasure hunting straight away, but luckily the mask trick kept me busy.

"Now, I have a couple of questions for you. Why did you tell the police you saw Heinrich leaving the barn? I feel sure you didn't really."

"You're right. I wanted Heinrich to fall into the trap of admitting in front of the police that he'd been into the barn and attacked Klaus. Without that, we'd have had no proof." Kotter whistled in admiration. "And what's your second question?"

"If you knew I'd come to St Antonio to get my hands on the treasure, why didn't you tell the police that?"

"Tell them what?" Dora winked at him. "The telltale footprints have already melted under the sun. And…"

"And what? Please don't keep me in suspense – I'm a sensitive soul, after all."

"Sensitive and sensible, I hope."

He looked at her quizzically.

"You're too clever to assume all this happened by mere chance. You returned to Val di Fleres, discovered a Neo Nazi who was the descendent of your grandfather's torturer, found this community's most precious treasure, and finally… let me spell it out frankly. You didn't show much talent as a thief. No, I don't call this pure chance at all."

"What do you call it?"

"It's Christmas, so I will simply call it redemption. It's the start of your new life."

THE END

Dear Reader,

Would you like to linger in the Christmas spirit? You can choose between a trip to a quaint Danish island in the Baltic sea with *"An Aero Island Christmas Mystery"* or head south for a Mediterranean December in *"A Mystery Before Christmas"*.

If you want to read more of Etta and Dora's adventures, why not start with **"The Watchman of Rothenburg Dies"**, the first book in *The Homeswappers Mysteries* series? Find out how a woman who swore never to allow a pet into her heart was won over and adopted by the proudest (and most adorable) of Basset Hounds. You can enjoy a free excerpt at the end of this book.

AUTHOR'S NOTE

Malga
This is a term only used in the Alps for a farm that is also a mountain hut welcoming guests. At times, a malga is only open for meals; at times it provides accommodation too.

IS SOUTHERN TYROL ITALIAN OR AUSTRIAN?
Southern Tyrol has officially been a part of Italy since 1918, but nowadays, this autonomous province has two official languages, German and Italian. Most places have two names, but since my ladies are from Southern Italy, I've used the Italian version of the names. In some cases, I have even adapted those for English readers.

Colle Isarco is also called Gossensass.

Vipiteno is Sterzing.

Even the mountains like the Parete Bianca (White Wall) is also called Weisswand, while the Cima del Tempo (Mountain of Time) is in fact the Wetterspitze.

I've also created an Italian-British "hybrid" for the village of St Antonio. In Italian, this would be Sant'Antonio or S Antonio, but I didn't want readers to wonder what that lonely "S" stood for. At the same time, I didn't want to turn it completely into the English "St Anthony", mostly to save you trouble. Should you ever decide, after having enjoyed the story, to visit Val di Fleres and you were to ask for directions to "St Anthony", most locals would look at you with blank faces.

The Holy Child statue

This statue is purely fictitious. To the best of my knowledge, there's never been such a silver statue, but in Colle Isarco, there's a chapel dedicated to St Barbara, the protector of miners, built with donations from both mine lords and their workers. Inside, one can still find the coats of arms from the different miners' guilds, and on the Gothic altar, the tiles are painted with scenes from miners' lives.

From this evidence of such a deep devotion, I felt it wasn't a big stretch to imagine that the miners might have made a silver statue of the Holy Child as a gift to their village church in St Antonio. As for the choice of silver, this was the most precious metal found in Val di Fleres, which in the eighteenth century was also known as the Silver Valley.

Ibsen in Colle Isarco

As Dora said, the famous Norwegian playwright, Henrik Johan Ibsen (b. 1828, d. 1906 in Norway), loved this part of Italy so much, he returned to Colle Isarco seven times, often staying at Grand Hotel Gröbner. He'd enjoy long walks in the morning and would write in the evening. A nice legend has him rinsing his ink pen in the village fountain every morning.

It was in Colle Isarco that the playwright met Emilie Bardach, a young woman who'd have a deep influence on his work. The main square has been dedicated to him and part of the town hall has become a museum and documentation centre for those curious to know more about the author.

Franz Hofer, the Tyrol *Gauleiter*

Franz Hofer was the most powerful Nazi party chief (*Gauleiter*) in Tyrol from 1938 until the end of the war, reporting directly to Hitler and Göring. You may think I'm referring to him when I mention the high-ranking Nazi in my story, but since I've found no evidence that he was involved in looting local treasures as other Nazi officials did, I decided not to use his name in the story. The Nazi that Heinrich is descended from is purely fictitious.

The Fortezza Treasure, on the other hand, is real. The Italian gold reserves were basically handed over to the Germans in 1943 when they were transferred from the bank vaults in Rome to Milan. The only condition Vincenzo Azzolini, the bank governor, could negotiate, after many arduous days of correspondence and meetings, was that the Bank of Italy would still own one of the three keys to access the reserves.

In December 1943, the gold had to be moved again, this time to Fortezza in Southern Tyrol (under Franz Hofer) as Göring felt this would be a safer place in case the Allies made their way to Milan. Azzolini attempted to find reasons not to move the reserves, but the pressure from the Nazis was simply too strong. Never supported by Mussolini in his objections, Azzolini finally convinced the Nazis they should let him know the exact location the treasure was to be moved to and that Italian security services would be used to guard it beside the Nazi soldiers.

In January 1944, Göring was already asking to move part of the treasure from Fortezza to Berlin as a contribution to the joint military effort. The news somehow reached the partisans – maybe Azzolini condoned this leak of information, even if he was not directly responsible for it – who bombed the railway lines north of Fortezza to stop the transfer. However, they only gained a few weeks' delay as this and other transfers of treasure were organised by the Nazis later on.

Azzolini kept track of at least some of the transfers, but on 1 August 1944, he was fired as the bank governor and arrested because he had collaborated with the Fascists in handing the Italian gold reserves over to the Nazis. Only in 1948 did the Italian Court of Justice, in a more serene atmosphere, recognise the man as not guilty.

After the war, two-thirds of the reserves were returned to Italy, as agreed by the Allies, but there's still great speculation about the rest of the loot. Some of the gold bullion may still be hidden in secret and unknown locations.

MORE BOOKS FROM ADRIANA LICIO

AN ITALIAN VILLAGE MYSTERY SERIES
0 - And Then There Were Bones. The prequel to the *An Italian Village Mystery* series is **available for free by signing up to www.adrianalicio.com/murderclub**

1 - Murder on the Road Returning to her quaint hometown in Italy following the collapse of her engagement, feisty travel writer Giò Brando just wants some peace and quiet. Instead, she finds herself a suspect in a brutal murder.

2 A Fair Time for Death The annual Chestnut Fair brings visitors from far and wide to the sleepy village of Trecchina. This year, one will be coming to die.

3 - A Mystery Before Christmas A haunting Christmas song from a faraway land. A child with striking green eyes. A man with no past.

4 - Peril at the Pellicano Hotel – A group of wordsmiths, a remote hotel. Outside, the winds howl and the seas rage. But the real danger lurks within.

5 - The Haunted Watch Tower – The doors are locked, the windows shuttered, but still he comes. Dare you set foot in the haunted watchtower?

THE HOMESWAPPERS MYSTERIES SERIES

Travelling Europe one... corpse at a time!

0 - Castelmezzano, The Witch Is Dead – Prequel to the series

1 - **The Watchman of Rothenburg Dies: A German Travel Mystery**

2 - **A Wedding and A Funeral in Mecklenburg : A German Cozy Mystery**

3 - **An Aero Island Christmas Mystery: A Danish Cozy Mystery**

4 – Prague, A Secret From The Past: A Czech Travel Mystery

5 – **Death on the West Highland Way: A Scottish Cozy Mystery**

6 – **The Ghost of Glengullion Castle: A Murder Mystery based in Scotland**

***

An Anthology: *A Christmas Mystery in Venice and Other Winter Tales – 3 Short Stories*

More books to come!

ABOUT THE AUTHOR

Adriana Licio lives in the Apennine Mountains in southern Italy, not far from Maratea, the seaside setting for her first cosy series, *An Italian Village Mystery*.

She loves loads of things: travelling, reading, walking, good food, small villages, and home swapping. A long time ago, she spent six years falling in love with Scotland, and she has never recovered. She now runs her family perfumery, and between a dark patchouli and a musky rose, she devours cosy mysteries.

She resisted writing as long as she could, fearing she might get carried away by her fertile imagination. But one day, she found an alluring blank page and the words flowed in the weird English she'd learned in Glasgow.

Adriana finds peace for her restless, enthusiastic soul by walking in nature with her adventurous golden retriever Frodo and her hubby Giovanni.

Do you want to know more?
Join the **Maratea Murder Club**

You can also stay in touch on:
www.adrianalicio.com

        facebook.com/adrianalicio.mystery
        twitter.com/adrianalici
        amazon.com/author/adrianalicio
        bookbub.com/authors/adriana-licio

THE MYSTERY BEFORE CHRISTMAS

AN ITALIAN VILLAGE MYSTERY

1 DECEMBER - A STEAMY CLAYPOT

"Mum, isn't this place the most beautiful in the world?" said young Betta, looking at the Maratea gulf from the bench on which she was sitting with her mother.

"Indeed it is."

"They have the mountains, they have the sea, can't we stay and live here?"

"I'm afraid we can't, young lady. I'd say it's time to move on to Naples."

"Oh, Mum, just another ten minutes. Look at the little houses over there. Wouldn't it be a dream to own one?"

"We'd better go, Betta, but I promise we will come back. You know, from Naples all we have to do is jump on a train to visit Maratea any time we want. And we will have Capri and Ischia nearby, and Sorrento. You'll love it there too."

But Anna didn't believe what she was saying herself. Like her daughter, she wished she could live in a quiet little village by the sea, but she needed to find a job. The opportunities the big city offered would allow her to earn enough to live a simple but decent life. That's what she hoped, at least. Life without Alex hadn't been easy so far.

"Come on, let's go." Anna took hold of Betta's hand and they headed towards the car. But when she climbed into the driver's seat and started the engine, it gave a feeble little murmur and died.

"What's wrong with it now?" Anna tried again, two, three times, but the engine's murmur was getting more feeble with each attempt until it ceased completely. The car simply wouldn't start.

Just what I need! Anna thought, trying to quell her rising anguish.

A woman she and Betta had exchanged a few words with in the central square stopped by to enquire if they needed help.

"Oh, thank you for asking, my car won't start. Do you know where I can find a garage?"

The woman shook her head. "It's Saturday afternoon, I'm afraid you'll have to wait until Monday."

"Monday!" Anna shrieked in horror. "Maybe it's only the battery. If someone would just help me to get it started, we'll be on our way to Naples."

The woman didn't look convinced. "I don't know much about cars, but if there's a problem, I'd say you'd better wait for it to be fixed. Imagine if you were to break down on the highway – it would be far more expensive to be picked up and towed away from there."

Expensive? How I loathe the very word. Anna's dark brown eyes opened wide in dismay, making her little face look even smaller and paler than usual.

"You'll need a place for the night," said the woman, as if reading Anna's mind. "I rent a small flat out to tourists in the high season, but at this time of year things are quiet, so I will only charge you for the heating and linen." She said her price and Anna breathed again; in Naples, accommodation would have cost so much more.

"Let's fetch your bags from the boot, it's just a short walk from here. I will ask my husband to call Nico, the mechanic, and see if he can have a look at your car. He may be able to do it tomorrow, but it's more likely to be on Monday."

"That's so very kind of you." But Anna felt embarrassed at being completely dependent on a stranger's kindness.

"Are we really sleeping here?" Betta asked the woman.

"You are. Do you like this town?"

"I love it!" Betta replied, a wide grin crossing her freckled face.

"My name is Nennella, by the way, and I own the newsstand on the other side of the town."

Betta and Anna introduced themselves and fetched their bags from the car. The apartment was in a little cobbled alley. It was cold inside, but Nennella switched on the heaters as soon as they were through the door.

"It will get very warm in a couple of hours," she said, showing them around. Then, looking more closely at Betta, she added, "This young one has very shiny eyes. You've not got a fever, have you?" She pressed her cheek against Betta's forehead, and then turned to Anna. "You'd better put her to bed."

Anna looked at her daughter; the woman was right. Betta had burning cheeks and bright, watery eyes.

"Oh, Betta, how do you feel?"

"I'm fine, Mum, I really am. I'm so happy we're staying here for the night."

"I'll fetch you a hot water bottle," said Nennella. "I live not far from here. In the meantime, make yourself comfortable."

After showing them where the towels and linen were, she left the young mother and feverish little girl alone.

BETTA WAS SLEEPING, BREATHING HEAVILY AS SHE DID WHEN SHE WAS sick. Anna had made up the beds, unpacked their things from their bags, and now she was sitting next to a heater to warm up a little, feeling helpless. She had left Aunt Battistina's home in Calabria; her aunt was the last living relative she had. And now here she was, stuck in the middle of nowhere. Was she mad?

The whole plan had been plain stupid; the most sensible thing to do would be to go back to her aunt. At the thought, though, Anna pushed her head against Betta's blankets and burst into silent tears, clenching her teeth to hold back her sobs so she wouldn't wake up her daughter.

She needed to buy some food, but she doubted the shops would still be open. She'd have to ask at a restaurant for a takeaway. As the practicalities filled her mind, she wiped her tears away.

The doorbell rang. Roundish and bubbly, Nennella came in, followed by Biagio, her quiet, lanky husband. He held a steaming red claypot in his hands while his wife did all the talking.

"This is a wholesome soup for you two. It will keep you warm and help your daughter recover too. And here is some bread and cheese and everything else you might need for tomorrow's breakfast." She moved into the kitchen, putting stuff in the fridge, the fruit basket, the bread box. "This is Doctor Tramutola's phone number, he is very good with kids. I told him you might need his services should Betta's temperature rise. He is old school and will come to see her tomorrow morning, if you need him to. Just call him early."

Anna felt so grateful, she was unable to speak. Stunned silence was actually the way most people reacted to Nennella's incessant chatter, but Anna wasn't to know that.

"I think you're all settled." Nennella touched Betta's forehead gently and added, "You shouldn't leave tomorrow, even if Nico can fix the car. This little one has a nasty fever."

Anna finally managed to get a word in edgeways. "Do you think we might stay here for one more night?"

"Not many tourists until we get closer to Christmas, so you can stay as long as you want, dear. But we'd better go, you look like you need a good rest too. I'll pop in tomorrow, and here's some paracetamol for Betta."

Biagio muttered something about the car and Anna handed him her keys. When the couple left, she felt like two angels had just passed by, leaving behind a heart-warming welcome and a red claypot from which the most delicious smell was coming.

2 DECEMBER – A ROBIN

"Nooooo!" A sharp cry resonated around the house. "Fernando, Fernando, come in here. Please!"

Mr Orlando joined his wife. "What has happened?"

"My pendant has gone!" his wife cried, showing him the empty case.

"Maybe you put it somewhere else last night," he said, doing his best to disguise his fear. The woman showed him the broken window pane.

"Someone broke in! They stole it!"

"Oh my goodness, how could they have known exactly how to get in?" Mr Orlando went outside. The little balcony could be reached by dropping down from the solid guttering. It wasn't an easy manoeuvre, but it wasn't impossible either. "We'd better call the carabinieri."

∼

THE DOORBELL RANG.

"Good morning, I'm just calling in to make sure you're fine and you've got all you need," Nennella said.

"Please, come in," Anna replied. As Nennella accepted the invitation and followed her into the small but sparklingly clean living room, she added, "The doctor came early this morning. I decided to call him even though she's only got a slight fever now, just to be on the safe side."

"You're right, better safe than sorry. And Dr Tramutola is such a comfort, isn't he?" Nennella said, sitting down on a chair next to the table, her eyes inspecting the spotless crystal chandelier above her head. Not one single grain of dust was allowed to settle in her presence.

"Indeed, he is a good man," Anna replied. She couldn't help following Nennella's gaze up to the ceiling as she continued speaking. "He approved the dose of paracetamol, but he says there's nothing to worry about. Just a cold with a bit of a fever, and if the fever has come down tomorrow, she can go out as normal the day after."

"I'm pleased to hear that. Kids can go from feverish to healthy in a couple of days, can't they? I'm just glad my flat was empty so I could help you out. Now you won't mind me doing this," she said, putting a newspaper on the sturdy wooden chair where she had been sitting, and climbing on top of it. A handkerchief in her hand, she polished the chandelier's three crystal flowers, each one holding a lightbulb, until they shone, chirping away merrily the whole time as if she were sitting comfortably on the sofa. "Also, the mechanic has taken a look at your car. It would seem the battery is rather old and needs to be replaced, but as it's Sunday, he can't get a new one until tomorrow. You wouldn't have gone far in that car."

"Oh, I don't know how to thank you…"

"No need for that. But I have to admit, I am a nosey lady," she said, landing on the floor, removing the newspaper from the chair and finally sitting down. "Would it be very rude if I were to ask you if you're all alone?"

"Of course not." Anna gave a look towards the bedroom;

Betta was sound asleep. "Yes, we are alone. Alex, my husband, passed away two years ago. We lived in Milan at the time. After his death, I tried to make ends meet, but the cost of living is rather high there."

"Did you have a job? And how did you manage with Betta?"

"Yes, I had a job at the reception of a private clinic. It paid enough to keep the two of us going. Also, I had a kind neighbour who helped me, watching Betta when I was at work. But she fell sick and had to go into a home for the elderly, and I wasn't earning enough to pay for a childminder too. Betta is a very responsible child, but she's too young to be left alone all day. I have one relative, an aunt on my mother's side, who lives in Calabria. She invited us to stay with her, and I knew life would be cheaper down south." Anna stopped.

"And have you now left her home?" Nennella asked without missing a beat.

Anna sighed. "It might sound rather ungrateful, but I didn't like life there. Aunt Battistina is a strong character and she wanted to control our lives entirely. Even if I was using my own money, she'd complain we were living on her charity. Also, I couldn't find any kind of work for myself, while Auntie was far too harsh with Betta."

Anna didn't mention how mean Aunt Battistina had been towards her too, nor did she refer to the woman's strict religious doctrines and the absurd rules she'd imposed on mum and daughter.

"It couldn't last. Though, in all truth, right now I'm not sure I've made the wisest choice. I hope I'll find a job in Naples, and a way to keep Betta safe when she's not at school."

"Well, in all honesty, I don't think going to Naples on your own, without knowing anyone there, is a great idea. But we will sort something out. One of the reasons I popped by was to ask if you want me to look after Betta, in case you need to go out for a while."

"I do want to buy something for lunch and dinner, so that would be very kind of you."

"The small mini-market in the main square is open in the mornings on a Sunday, and there's a trattoria at the end of this alley if you want to fetch a takeaway. Off you go, now."

∽

IT WAS LATE AFTERNOON WHEN GIÒ BRANDO ENTERED HER SISTER'S perfumery. She looked around, her green eyes showing her disappointment.

"At least you have a few Christmas things out. But there's nothing in the village at all. That's a shame!"

"But it's the tradition here, you know that," Agnese reminded her sister. "Christmas officially starts on the eighth of December."

The two women couldn't have looked more different. Agnese's face was a perfect oval with distinctively Mediterranean features and intense dark eyes. Her slightly plump figure was smartly dressed in skirt and blouse. Giò, on the other hand, was tall with short dark hair, her boyish figure sporting jeans, fitted jacket and a colourful scarf.

"But that's too late! The festivities will be over before they've even started." Giò was spending her first Christmas in her hometown after having lived in the UK for a number of years. She had broken up with her fiancé just before the wedding was due to take place and decided to go back home after having spent a decade in London, trying to keep him happy. Dorian Gravy had always hated Maratea so she had given up spending Christmases at home. Deep in her heart, she had always missed them, but now she felt disappointed. In the UK, the Christmas season would have started just after Halloween. On the streets of Maratea, it was now December and there were still no Christmas lights, no Christmas trees, and only a handful of shops displaying cheerful seasonal decorations.

"Well, I try to get started on the first December in the shop," Agnese said, pointing to the windows which were festooned with red ribbons and felt decorations.

"But it's Sunday, your shop is open and there's virtually no one around."

"The first Sunday of the month is always like that, but it's fine by me. I have so much work to do." Agnese pointed to a number of boxes next to the counter, "I don't mind having a little time to prepare it all."

"I don't know – the weather is warm, the sun is shining. It doesn't look like Christmas at all."

"How's your writing going?" asked Agnese, suspecting her sister's blue mood was due more to personal reasons than a lack of decorations in the streets.

"I've done my first draft and I'm starting the edits," Giò answered, waving her hand as if dismissing a nightmare. "I thought I'd celebrate with a Christmas walk…"

"Sorry, but you'll have to wait." Agnese chuckled before adding, "And at home, Granny won't allow you to get the Christmas tree up until the eighth of December, as tradition dictates."

"I'm planning on buying one for my flat, just a little one, but I'm not sure I will find it today. It seems as though everyone in Maratea is determined to ignore the fact that it's Christmas."

"The good news is that this year, to allow businesses to enjoy a full working day on the eighth of December, Mayor Zucchini has decided the Christmas lights will be turned on on the evening of the seventh, in time for the official start of the festivities." With a grin, Agnese added, "You're getting an extra half day of Christmas."

But Giò just shrugged and left her sister's perfumery. She needed a walk, decorations or no decorations. Editing was tough for her; it required attention to all manner of minutiae, something her temperamental nature wasn't too keen on. She walked to the Villa Comunale, the public garden almost at the end of the village, and there sat on a bench. As it was nearly dark, the yellow lamps were on. The damp of the grass and the trees made her shiver a bit; this was the closest she'd get to a Christmas atmosphere for the day.

A little robin stood on the branches above her head. He was bobbing up and down, indifferent to the encroaching darkness, giving out a little chirp every now and then.

"Aren't you out a bit late? Anyway, I'm glad you're enjoying yourself."

Giò rested her head against a tree trunk, breathing in the light scent of damp moss. She closed her eyes and imagined a traditional Christmas scene with snow, kids singing, streets shining with lights, a Christmas Market and the scent of mulled wine in the air.

"*The carillon!*" murmured a voice.

Giò's eyes flew open and she looked around, startled. There was nobody in view. The little bird bowed his head and disappeared up to the higher branches, maybe to his nest.

Who spoke? Did I dream it? Giò wondered. *Carillon* – it was ages since she'd last heard that word, used in Italy to refer to any sort of musical box. *Time to go home. Never mind Christmas lights, it looks like I'm getting Christmas hallucinations.*

3 DECEMBER – A MISSING BOOK

Agnese was opening the boxes the courier had just delivered, containing a collection of candles she had ordered in for Christmas. They were no ordinary candles; they were of the finest quality, made from six different types of beeswax. This would allow them to burn slowly, and as they warmed up, they would release the perfume they contained. No commercial fragrance, this was a real perfume composed by a true perfume master – first the head or starting notes, then the middle or heart ones, and finally the back notes. A heart-warming tale coming to life under your very nose. The candles had not been cheap and Agnese hoped her customers would appreciate their beauty, including the stunning handmade ceramic pots they sat in.

The doorbell rang as Nennella came in. The chatty woman actually stopped on the threshold to read the notice Agnese had posted on her door.

'*Christmas help needed.*'

She then smiled. "Good morning, Agnese."

"Good morning, Nennella. Please do come in."

"I'm glad to see this," the older woman indicated the notice.

Then looking around, she added, "I imagine you've not found anybody yet."

"Exactly, each year it seems to get more difficult."

"How about Giò, can't she help you?"

"She will in the last-minute rush up to Christmas... but she has work to finish by early January, and I need full-time help." Agnese showed Nennella the number of boxes she had waiting to be opened, all full of items needing to be checked, inventoried and priced, their details inserted onto the sales software.

"Well, I might have the right person for you," and Nennella told her about Anna.

"Poor souls. Such a sad story, but wouldn't it be better for them to go on to Naples as soon as they can so the little girl can get started in school?"

"Big city, I guess she won't be allowed to start in a new school until after the Christmas holidays. In Maratea, she can start tomorrow – I've already spoken to the teachers. Also, at Christmas, a lot of people return here from Naples to visit family. They might be able to help Anna find a cheap flat, not to mention a job."

"And you think she might be willing to help me in the shop?"

"She'd love that. She is a sensible, trustworthy young woman, she's longing to work, and I believe... she's your type."

Agnese laughed at that. "I didn't know I had a type."

"Well, there's something different about this shop of yours. It's never been like any other in town. You're very practical in some respects, but it's clear this is more than just a business for you. Anna, for some reason, seems to be cut from the same cloth as you. Would you like to meet her?"

"Of course. Tell her to come in this afternoon, before opening time."

Anna entered Piazza Vitolo, the square in front of Maratea Town Hall, and looked around to find the alley on the right-hand side that Nennella had mentioned. Spotting a sign displaying the perfumery name, she walked in that direction and stopped in front of windows framed in turquoise wood. Peering curiously through the windows and liking what she saw, she moved towards the door and saw the notice.

It was the right place.

A nice smell of smoky wood, pine needles and sage welcomed her as she walked through the door, looking around.

"Hello, can I help you?" Agnese said.

"Good morning, Mrs Fiorillo, I'm Anna Giordano. Nennella told me I could come to have a chat with you." But as she spoke, Anna's eyes continued to wander around. She couldn't help herself – the place was beyond fantastic. She had imagined a modern perfumery, but this was something totally different.

White and turquoise cabinets and old bookcases displayed perfume bottles and toiletries. A vintage letterpress on the wall was filled with soaps from Portugal in vibrant colours, while in the centre of the room, an ebony table displayed gift sets especially for Christmas along with candles and, at its feet, beautiful white lanterns from Sweden, pillows with snowflake designs and fleece blankets patterned with forest creatures.

"This is beautiful," Anna said with such simplicity, Agnese had no doubt she was sincere.

"Glad you like it." Then, seeing Anna sniffing the air and looking around again, Agnese added, "And no, there's no fireplace. It's just that winter candle giving off the scent of burned wood and pine needles."

"It feels so cosy!" Anna smiled. "I really thought there must be a fireplace somewhere." She paused, as if to remind herself she was not there to shop. "Maybe I'm chatting too much. I came because Nennella told me you are looking for a sales assistant for the Christmas season."

"Have you any experience of working in a shop?"

"I'm afraid not, but I am willing to learn." Anna looked up at the boxes near the computer, then at Agnese entering the items one by one into the sales software. "And I'm quite good with computer stuff."

"Oooh, I'd love a hand with this. It's the part I struggle with most."

"If you just show me how to do it once, I'll be glad to help."

"That will be very useful. Over the next few days, we will need to get ready for the rush. After the eighth of December, we'll mostly be concentrating on sales and gift wrapping."

"I did a course on paper craft, so I might be able to help with that as well. But I'm afraid I'm not familiar with perfumes and creams and make-up."

"Nor were the helpers I got in for Christmas in the past." Agnese smiled. "Let's start by sorting out that stuff near the counter. Do you think you can spare an hour to work with me now?"

"I certainly can. But I do have a young daughter. I don't know how, but Nennella convinced the school to let her join classes from tomorrow. In the afternoons, would you mind if she stayed here with me during working hours? She's very quiet."

"I've got a daughter too, about the same age I believe. Lilia is eight."

"Betta turned eight in August."

"They could do their homework together in the afternoons. My grandma will watch over them."

"That'd be perfect." Anna smiled, knowing how much Betta would love to have a new friend – particularly a friend in Maratea.

Agnese showed Anna how the software worked. The young woman learned fast and fed the details of all the new candles and gift sets into the system far more quickly than Agnese could have managed it. As Nennella had guessed, Anna was an uncomplicated but efficient soul.

"I think we can stop here for today since you've left your little girl with Nennella," Agnese said, going on to inform Anna about pay and working hours. Anna replied she had no need to think it over – she was glad to accept the job offer and start work the next morning.

∼

"M<small>RS</small> L<small>IBRETTO</small>, I <small>CAN'T FIND</small> M<small>ATILDA</small>, <small>THE BOOK YOU READ TO US</small> last Saturday. Did someone borrow it?" Luca asked, his dark eyes extremely serious.

Laura Libretto, Maratea's librarian, smiled at the boy in front of her. "I don't think so," she said, checking on the computer. "The book should be here. Maybe someone just put it back in the wrong place."

They went through the books on the returns trolley together, then looked on the children's shelves of the library. Mrs Libretto checked the more popular adult sections, just in case a distracted father or mother had dropped it there while searching for their own favourite books. Nothing.

"It seems it's not here, but I'm sure it will pop up when I sort out the other books. Some readers are rather careless. I'll drop it off at your mother's shop if it turns up. In the meantime, why don't you read *Charlie and the Chocolate Factory*?"

"I loved Matilda's superpowers, but I will give this a go," Luca said, taking the book she was handing to him and going to sit in the reading room.

Mrs Libretto watched him sit down and start reading quietly next to Tommaso, an older man who was fond of philosophy. As for herself – well, in all honesty, she was rather worried. *Matilda* wasn't the first book to have gone missing from the library in the last few weeks.

4 DECEMBER – A STARTLING RESEMBLANCE

"Good afternoon, madam, is there anything I can do for you?" Anna asked politely. An older lady, her slight figure dressed all in black, had just entered the shop.

"Yes, dear, I'm looking for ideas. Christmas is coming, and though I'm not fond of buying presents, there are a few people I can't neglect."

Anna asked what kind of presents she was looking for, and then they started to go through the numerous options the shop offered for the festive season.

"Isn't Agnese in today?"

"She's just gone to run a quick errand, she should be back any minute. Do you want me to call her?"

"No, not at all. You're very helpful too, it's just strange not to see her."

"She'll be back soon."

The door opened and Lilia and Betta came in. Lilia, as self-confident as ever, came forward and spoke to the customer.

"Good afternoon, Mrs De Blasi."

"Hello, Lilia, you're growing up fast. I almost didn't recognise you."

Lilia swelled with pride.

"Are you with a friend?" Mrs De Blasi indicated Betta, who was lingering at the entrance.

"This is my daughter," Anna said, calling Betta forward. "Betta, come over to say hello."

As the child came forward, Mrs De Blasi froze. The green eyes under a fringe of dark blonde hair; the little nose and the curve of the mouth; even the scattering of freckles across Betta's face. The older woman staggered and Anna had to catch her and help her to sit down on a nearby seat.

At that moment, the doorbell tinkled and Agnese came in, surprised to find two scared girls, a woman fainting on one of her armchairs, and Anna looking beyond relieved to see her.

"Please, Agnese, get Mrs De Blasi a glass of water with two spoonfuls of sugar."

When she had drunk the sugary water down, some colour returned to Mrs De Blasi's face. "I'm so sorry," she murmured.

"How do you feel? Do you want me to call a doctor?"

"No, not at all. I'm feeling better now." She searched the room with her eyes, stopping only when they lighted upon Betta. "Would you remind this silly old lady what your name is?"

"Elisabetta," Betta stuttered, feeling rather self-conscious as the attention of everyone present was on her.

"Oh my goodness!" Mrs De Blasi went rigid, looking even paler than she had when she'd felt faint. Agnese and Anna looked at each other in confusion. What was going on here?

(...)

Keep reading *"The Mystery Before Christmas" - Book 3 in The Italian Village Msytery series can be enjoyed as part of the series or as a standalone.*

www.ingramcontent.com/pod-product-compliance
Lightning Source LLC
LaVergne TN
LVHW041840070526
838199LV00045BA/1363